MISTAKEN

By

Laurel Joseph

©2008 by Laurel Joseph and Blushing Books

Copyright © 2008 by Blushing Books ® and Laurel Joseph

All rights reserved. No part of the book may be reproduced or transmitted in any form or by any means, electronic or mechanical, including photocopying, recording, or by any information storage and retrieval system, without permission in writing from the publisher.

Published by Blushing Books ®,
a subsidiary of
ABCD Graphics and Design
977 Seminole Trail #233
Charlottesville, VA 22901

The trademark Blushing Books ® is registered in the US Patent and Trademark Office.

Laurel Joseph
    Mistaken
ISBN 978-1-935152-06-4

Cover Design: Rae Monet

This book is intended for adults only. Spanking and other sexual activities represented in this book are fantasies only, intended for adults. Nothing in this book should be interpreted as advocating any non-consensual spanking activity or the spanking of minors. All characters or fictional and no resemblance between any persons, living or dead, is intended or implied.

Thank you for purchasing this copy of Mistaken by Laurel Joseph

Please check out our websites sites, including Spanking Romance, located at http://www.spankingromance.com. A completed novel or novella is published here each week.
We also operate Bethany's Woodshed, located at (http://www.herwoodshed.com) the Internet's oldest and largest spanking story site. In operation since 1998, Bethany's has published hundreds of full length spanking romances, all professionally written. Please check out our website for more wonderful stories by Laurel Joseph and other fine authors.
We also run an eBook site at Romantic Spankings (http://www.romanticspankings.com). Here you will find hundreds of eBooks for immediate download.
Our print book site is located at SpankBooks. (http://www.spankbooks.com)
If you own an Kindle eBook reading device, marketed by Amazon.com, you can see what books we have available for the Kindle at http://www.spanking4mykindle.com

For other fiction by Laurel Joseph visit:
http://www.JoannieWrites.com

Chapter One

"Of all the irresponsible, hair-brained stunts!" Wesley roared, his temper raging within him as he swept off his hat and slapped it against his thighs, revealing a thick crop of wavy, red hair. "What the *hell* do you think you are doing here?"

Jolie looked around the crowded saloon, wondering who the tall cowboy was speaking to. He seemed to be addressing *her*, but she'd never set eyes on the man before.

"I never thought I'd see the day when I'd see my *wife* in a damned saloon!" he ranted, grabbing Jolie's slender wrist and jerking her to her feet. "Playing poker and sipping beer! By God, you need a hiding, and you're sure as sin gong to get it!"

"Let me go!" Jolie tried to jerk free but the man was simply too strong. She'd heard that demented souls possessed extra strength, and surely this man was crazy! "I am not your wife!" she hissed, and then kicked him as hard as possible. "Let me go, damn it!"

In a matter of seconds, the green eyes regarding her so steadily changed from temper-filled to enraged and foreboding.

"Swearing! Kicking! My God, I don't *believe* this!"

Jolie found herself jerked closer, and before she could fathom his intentions, she found herself dangling over his left arm while his right hand slapped heartily on the seat of her well-worn britches.

"Ow! Stop! Stop!" she yelled. "Someone, help me, please! Oh, ow!"

"How dare you, Jacy? How dare you pull a stunt like this?" the madman continued to spank her over and over, and Jolie was positive her britches were smoking from the fire inside them!

"I am *not* Jacy!" she screamed. "Please, someone *help* me! Ow! Ow! Ow!"

"I'll teach you to trail after me like this, Jacy Parker!" the cowboy promised, delivering the worst spanking she'd ever had in all her life.

"I don't know any Jacy Parker!" Jolie yelled. "Stop! Stop! Stop!" her legs kicked wildly.

"Good Lord, Wes! Put that girl down!" another male voice spoke up.

"Jacy is *my* wife, Drew. Don't be tellin' me what to do!"

"Wes! This girl isn't Jacy," Drew grabbed his brother's hand to stop the punishment. "Look at her left hand. No wedding band, and you know as well as I do, Jacy wouldn't ever take off your ring. And if she did, there'd be a streak of white around her finger. This girl isn't Jacy..."

"No, I'm not this Jacy person!" Jolie declared tearfully, barely able to resist the urge to rub her stinging posterior while standing in front of all these men.

The man called Wes stared at her intently for a few unnerving seconds, then picked up her left hand to look at her ring finger. Shock filled his eyes, then his cheeks turned a flaming red to surpass his red hair! "You really aren't my Jacy!" he whispered in awe.

"You owe this girl an apology, little brother," Drew stated matter-of-factly, staring at Jolie.

"Yes, I do," Wes mumbled to himself, and then asked, "Who are you, Miss? And what the heck are you doing in a saloon, wearing men's britches and drinking beer?" His tone of voice suggested the whole incident was Jolie's fault.

"I can't see where it's any of *your* business…!" she pointed out, and then made short work of picking up her winnings from the table and shoving the money in her pockets.

"Girl, what's your name?" the one called Drew asked in a tone of voice that suggested he was used to being obeyed.

She looked him up and down with her blue eyes, then turned on her booted heel and headed for the swinging doors. She had no intention of telling these two *anything*!

Drew moved to stand in front of the door, then spoke in a conciliatory manner, "I know you're a bit peeved with Wes at the moment, girl, and you have a right to be… but you've got to be related to our Jacy. You look just like her!"

"For your information, I don't have *any* family, *anywhere*! Now let me pass."

"It's got to be her, Drew," Wes said in delight.

Drew nodded solemnly, and then said, "You're Jacy's twin sister, Jolie."

"You're just as crazy as he is," Jolie pointed at Wes. Her poor backside was simply on fire, and she needed to get out of here so she could tend to herself.

"I can sure as sin see why you'd think that," Wes spoke up, staring hard at her face, "But you've got to believe us. You're the spittin' image of my wife, Jacy. You've just got to be Jolie…?" Jolie's chin turned up, and Wes grinned at the stubborn gesture… "You even hold your head like Jacy does when she's bein' stubborn, and just beggin' for a trip to the woodshed!"

"I don't have no family. I told you that. Now get out of my way," the last was tossed in Drew's direction.

"Jolie, that IS your name, isn't it...?" Drew asked with a friendly smile.

"What if it is? Doesn't mean anything..." she quickly denied.

"It means that you have a sister who is dying to meet you," Drew responded in a quiet voice. "Would you please sit down with us, and give Wes a chance to tell you about Jacy? Then, if you still believe we're crazy, we'll let you go on your way without another word."

Jolie looked from one big man to the other. At small as she was, and without her gun, she wasn't going to get past them. She might as well hear them out, then hope that the other men in this saloon would help her escape if need be... or at least go for the Sheriff! She cocked her head, and then asked, "Buy me another beer?"

"You sure as sin shouldn't be drinking beer!" Wes scolded, his green eyes full of irritation.

"Wes, one beer isn't going to make a difference. I'm going to have one, too," Drew grinned at his younger brother. "You two pick a table and sit down."

Jolie flashed Wes a "so there too" look, and stomped across the room to take a seat at a table as far away from prying ears as possible. She turned one leg under her so that her smarting backside wouldn't make contact with the hard seat, and simply sat there and glared at Wes while waiting for Drew to return with her beer.

"You really are Jacy's sister," Wes announced solemnly. "You look just like her, except she has more sense than to look at me with that attitude."

"You beat her all the time?" Jolie asked sarcastically, and then added, "I feel sorry for the poor woman!"

"I don't beat her," Wes intoned as Drew walked over with three mugs of beer and sat them on the table. "But I sure don't put up with a lot of sass..."

Before Jolie could say anything else, Drew pointed at her beer. "Enjoy that beer, young lady. Might be the last one you get for a very long time."

Jolie nodded. She was flat broke, and having the devil's own time finding a job. "Let's hear what you have to say so that I can be on my way. There's no work to be had here, and I need to move on..."

"You're comin' home with us to meet your sister," Wes's green eyes glowered at her.

"Wes, your temper is getting the best of you again," Drew looked over his mug at his scowling brother. "Why not tell Jolie what you know...?"

Jolie looked at Drew. "You tell me, I don't trust the likes of him!" Her poor butt was still stinging, and she tried to reach back and rub without either of the cowboys guessing what she was up to.

"You can trust Wes," Drew told her seriously, then said, "If you'd be more comfortable standing right now...?"

Jolie felt her face turn red. "I'm just fine!" she sputtered indignantly.

"If you say so," Drew grinned, then warned, "You go tossing that beer at me, little girl, and you'll get another spanking, and I'm not as weak as my little brother."

"You go to lay a hand on me and I'll shoot you dead!" Jolie promised, forgetting that the Sheriff in the last town had confiscated her guns, telling her it was for her own good!

Wes looked at Drew. "She needs a switching or two..."

"I don't have to listen to this!" Jolie jumped to her feet and headed for the swinging doors. She didn't get more than a couple steps before she was grabbed from behind, swung around, and plopped on her chair with a thump.

"You are going to sit right there, and hear us out, little girl," Drew didn't raise his voice, yet Jolie heard the steel determination in his words. "Wes, tell her about Jacy," he ordered. When Jolie felt his grip relax, she twisted her arm free, and started to rise again.

"Guess I'll have to get your attention first," Drew easily caught her and hauled her back to the table.

Jolie gasped in outrage as he used his booted foot to pull her chair away from the table, and then sat down. In the next instant, she was face-down over his thighs, looking at the cracks in the wooden floor. "No!" she protested in vain just seconds before Drew's hand landed on the seat of her jeans. "Noooooooooo!" she kicked her legs. But Drew simply ignored her and spanked her poor bottom until she was crying.

"Do you think you can sit here now and listen to Wes?" Drew asked. When the little blonde nodded, he gave her one more resounding whack, and then lifted her to her feet. "You sure as heck do know how to try a man's patience, little girl." He pulled the chair to the table, and then motioned for her to sit.

Jolie bit her lip to keep from crying out as her tender backside made contact with the unrelenting wood. The last thing she felt like doing right now was sitting!

"Jacy is my wife," Wes started. "I met her about three years ago when Drew and I were scouting for a wagon train. She and her Ma, Abigail Clarkson, were traveling west with a group of settlers."

Drew didn't miss the way Jolie's eyes widened at the mention of Jacy's mother's name, and he was more positive than ever that she was Jacy's twin sister. The problem would be getting the stubborn little blonde to admit it.

"Jacy is a pretty little thing, and she finally agreed to marry me," Wes's eyes sparkled. "Jacy's Ma lived with us... But she wasn't very strong. We had an army doctor look at her, and he said she had a weak heart. She called us to her one night, and said she had to tell Jacy somethin' she'd kept from her for eighteen years. Seems that Jacy's Pa wasn't dead like she'd told

Jacy. He'd run off, and took Jacy's twin sister, Jolie, with him. Abby couldn't find them, even though she'd searched for years. She wanted Jacy to promise to keep lookin' for her sister, and Jacy promised she would. Abby died a couple days later..." He looked at Jolie, and then said, "I think you're Jacy's twin sister, and you're comin' home with Drew and me."

Jolie bristled at the words. "You can't tell me what to do!"

"Jolie," Drew demanded her attention. "Does any of what Wes said ring true with you?"

Jolie wasn't going to lie. "Pa's name was Zeke Clarkson. I was told my Ma died having me. Knowing Pa, and how mean he was, it sounds like something he would do. Your Jacy is twenty years old?" she asked Wes.

He nodded. "Her birthday is August 1," he added.

Jolie shook her head, and then smiled to herself. The fact she had a twin sister somewhere explained why she felt someone was missing from her life... She'd always thought it was her mother... but now she knew the truth. She had a sudden flash of memory, and she asked, "Did Jacy get hurt a couple years ago?"

Wes looked at Drew in shock, but then replied, "She fell off a horse and broke her arm..."

Jolie nodded. "It was her left arm. I felt it," she explained to them. "Was hunting for our supper at the time, and just spotted a rabbit. Scared it off by screaming in pain. Pa was furious with me." She got to her feet. "I need some time to think about this. I'll give you my answer in the morning."

Drew put out a hand to stop Wes from going after her. "Remember how Jacy felt when she learned about her sister. Didn't want to talk for a while, kept going for long walks alone...?"

"Yea, I remember. She didn't snap out of it until I turned her over my knee," Wes said glumly. "Couldn't believe that she would walk that far by herself and get lost!"

"You have a rotten temper, Wes," Drew shook his head.

"You just wait until you fall in love, brother. Your woman goes off by herself and gets lost and you can't find her for hours, and it's dark out there... You'd lose your temper and do some fanny burning, too!"

"Can't believe Jacy puts up with you!" Drew teased.

"I'm going to follow Jolie," Wes got to his feet. "I'm not goin' home and tell Jacy I found her sister, but let her get away."

Drew shook his head, but decided that Wes was probably right. He wouldn't want to face Jacy if they lost the girl.

****

Jacy left the town of Willow Creek behind her. She'd been on her own for a little over a year now, and she liked it that way just fine. Besides, what did she and her twin sister have in common? Nothing but their looks. Jacy sounded like a lady, and she was a drifter that lived mostly off the land, and what odd jobs she could find. She hadn't had a real home in more years than she could remember. Pa liked to keep moving.

She'd hated spending the last of her money to buy another gun, but what choice did she have? A girl had to eat... She spotted a rabbit, and smiled grimly when her aim was true. At least she wouldn't go hungry tonight.

She was getting the fire started when she heard riders approaching at a fast gallop. Experience had taught her to be wary and very careful of strangers... She'd pushed her long, blonde braid up under her hat before riding out of town, and with the oversized jacket covering her, she could pass for a boy. It was much safer to be a boy than a young woman all alone.

Still, she rested her hand on her gun, and kept it there, ready for trouble.

"You!" she spat the word. "Go away and leave me the hell alone!"

"We heard the shot," Drew explained, dismounting. "Thought you could have trouble." His dark eyes noted the fact she was wearing a gun with the holster strapped down.

"No trouble, but for you two. Go away," she ordered.

"We can't do that," Drew said softly before his brother could speak up. "Jacy would be upset if we came home without you."

"Like I give a damn," Jolie gave vent to her temper. "I'm not going with you."

"Yes, you are," Drew said decisively, and in the next second his hat flew off his head! The brat had shot at him! "You little hellion!" he growled menacingly. "You shot at me!"

"Don't be stupid!" Jolie scoffed. "If I'd shot at you, you'd be dead!"

Drew picked up his hat, and then poked his finger through the hole. He looked at her, the fury radiating from his dark eyes, and then tossed the hat on the ground.

Jolie's blue eyes widened in trepidation as he started for her, murder clearly on his mind. "You just stop right there!" she backed up a few steps. "I mean it! I wasn't shooting at YOU, just your hat!" she squeaked, and when that didn't stop his approach, she turned and fled on foot, wanting to put some distance between them.

Wes grinned wickedly when his brother gave chase. He had a feeling that Drew was about to learn first hand how a little girl could get under his skin; Drew might not know it yet, but he was hooked on Jolie. He calmly set about cleaning the rabbit, hoping his brother had enough sense to cut a switch this time.

****

Jolie prided herself on being able to run fast; very, very fast! But, unfortunately, Drew's legs were much longer than hers, and he was no slouch in the running department either. He was slowly overtaking her, and his eyes were still full of fury. She knew what that meant... and she didn't want a third spanking! Her poor backside was still aching from the other two, and it was all she could do to sit her saddle long enough to ride this far!

Drew wasn't about to let the little blonde hellion get away with shooting at him! He was going to take down her britches and set her cute little ass on fire! It was long past time someone took her in hand, and it seemed he was the one elected to do it. He added a bit more energy into catching her, and when he was just about close enough to catch her, he jumped and tackled her to the ground, careful not to hurt her in the process. She was tiny, like Jacy, and he didn't want to do more than dent that pride of hers in a manner that would make a lasting impression.

"Let me go!" Jolie screamed, kicking for all she was worth when he rolled her over to face him.

Drew trapped her legs by throwing his right leg over them. His left hand held both of her wrists above her head, and his right went to work unbuckling her gun belt, her belt, then fumbled with the buttons on her pants.

"What are you doing?" Jolie struggled even harder.

Drew could see the fear in her blue eyes. "I'm going to make sitting down a memory for you," he told her. "I'm going to make you sorry as hell you shot at me."

"No!! I wasn't shooing AT you!" she insisted. "I shot at your hat!"

"You don't point guns at people, little girl," Drew was livid. "You're going to learn that lesson the hard way." He tugged her pants down, and then undid the string holding up her drawers.

"No! No! No! Leave them on!" Jolie fought for her dignity, but lost. She was completely bare to his gaze, but far from being impressed with her womanly charms, Drew seemed oblivious to the blond curls covering her most private area. He easily flipped her over, and his right hand found her naked backside. "Owww!" Jolie cried out. "It hurts!" she wailed as he continued to pepper her with stinging spanks.

"It's supposed to hurt!" he told her. "I'm glad it hurts. I want it to hurt!" he added. Her cheeks quickly turned red, and Drew decided to make the backs of her thighs match. Her yells told him that she didn't find that particularly enjoyable, so he put some real effort in tanning her.

Drew was killing her, Jolie was positive of it! She hadn't been spanked in years... and this was the third time in one day... in less than three hours, in fact. She was in misery! "Please stop! I'm sorry... I'm sorry!" she said breathlessly.

"Not nearly sorry enough," Drew scolded, and proceeded to lecture her while he spanked her sit spot over and over again.

Jolie was crying in earnest by the time he stopped.

"Do I have your attention?" Drew demanded.

Jolie nodded miserably.

"Good. You're going to cut a switch, and prepare it," he took out his knife and held it out to her. "Make it a good one, or else I will cut one, and use it twice as long."

"Please don't!" Jolie was shocked he would even consider using a switch on her already sore bottom. "I'm too sore! I'm really sorry! I won't ever do it again," she pleaded.

"You sure won't do it again," he agreed, his dark eyes full of determination. "You have two choices here, Jolie. Either you cut that switch, and get it ready, and get twenty-five cuts with it... Or I cut it, prepare it, and you get fifty. Your choice, and you've got about five seconds to make your decision before I make it for you."

Jolie felt as though she'd butted up against a solid rock. The big cowboy wasn't going to change his mind. She was going to get a switching, and it was either going to be unbearable, or doubly unbearable. Reluctantly, she got to her feet, and waddled with her pants around her ankles, to the nearest tree. She looked for a bit, and then found a switch that seemed small enough, yet sturdy enough it wouldn't break. She had no doubt at all in her mind that she didn't want HIM to pick the switch.

Drew watched without the least bit of sympathy as the little blonde used his knife to strip the bark from the limb. He was going to raise some serious welts on that pretty little backside of hers, and teach her a valuable lesson. She simply could not go around shooting at people. The next man might take his fists to her, or even shoot her dead for such a thing. A striped backside might very well save her life. He could tell by the red flush on her cheeks that she was embarrassed at having to choose and prepare the switch, and he'd have to remember to thank Wes for the lesson. Poor little Jacy had been sent to do the same on several occasions, and Wes told him later that the added punishment did more to bring the lesson home than the stinging stripes he laid on her butt.

Jolie finished, and couldn't stall any longer. She handed Drew his knife, then put the switch in his hand. He continued to look at her, and she lowered her eyes to the ground.

"Why are you getting this switching, Jolie?" he demanded.

"Because I shot the hat off your head, and it was a dangerous thing to do," she admitted.

"See that rock?" he pointed with the switch. "I want your bare butt right on top of it."

"Please, Drew... I'm sorry! I won't do it again... I swear! I don't think I can take any more punishment..."

"You won't enjoy this, little girl, but you will take it, and you will remember it the next time you're tempted to shoot that gun in a fit of temper. Now bend over, and let's get this whipping over with."

Jolie wanted to run, but knew she wouldn't get very far with the pants around her ankles. She finally accepted the fact she was going to get her butt whipped with the switch, and there was no sense in making Drew any angrier than he already was. She went to the rock, and lay over the top of it. Her hands barely reached the ground on the other side, and her toes were off the ground. She would have no leverage whatsoever to get herself out of the way of the switch. Her poor butt and thighs were Drew's to do with as he wished.

Drew placed his left hand on the small of her back to steady her, and then brought the switch down over the reddened cheeks, leaving a red welt of fire behind. Jolie yelped. He laid the next one right below the first, and gave it time to register before applying the third.

Jolie was frantic. It hurt worse than she'd thought it would! "Please stop!" she begged, desperation in her voice. Drew ignored her. Her thighs were next to feel the sharp line of fire, and Jolie was unable to protect it from happening over and over again.

"You've had ten. Another fifteen to go," Drew told her.

"No, oh no! Oh Please, Drew... No more. I'll be good. I promise!"

"Amazing how a switching will change an attitude," Drew had the nerve to chuckle, then continued striping her butt, making sure the switch left a vivid mark each time. "That was five more, and you have ten left. They're all going to be in the same spot, Jolie, and you won't sit for a week without remembering this punishment and why it was given."

Jolie screamed when the switch bit into the most sensitive area of her bottom, her sit spot. Over and over and over, Drew brought the lesson home, and the last one of all was the most painful. Jolie was sobbing and limp by the time he finished.

Drew let her cry for a bit, and then lifted her to stand on her feet. Now that she was punished, it occurred to him that he was looking where he shouldn't be looking. "Cover yourself, young lady," he ordered gruffly, then finally helped her to do it when her hands were shaking too much to do so. He pulled her close and hugged her comfortingly. "I know you're hurting, Jolie, but you needed a sharp lesson. Don't you ever pull a gun on anyone again unless you're aiming to kill in self defense. Got that?" His hand swatted her lightly.

Jolie jumped, then said, "Yes, sir."

"Good girl," Drew said in approval. "Let's get you back to camp and see if brother has that rabbit cooking. I've worked up an appetite."

****

Jolie was getting scared. She didn't know why, but she expected it had to do with whether or not her sister would like her. She'd been raised by their mother, and was a lady, while she'd been raised by their father, and was far from being a lady. She wore pants, frequented saloons, and could shoot better than most men. Not that she was likely to pull her gun again anytime soon…

She glanced sideways at Drew, and sighed deeply. Sitting the last few days had been nearly impossible, thanks to the spanking and the switching he'd given her. In retrospect, she supposed she'd deserved it, but it still rankled that he'd bared her completely. She never wanted to go through that again. Drew simply didn't have the right to correct her.

The small ranch was perfect, Jolie decided when she got her first glimpse of the buildings. It was neat and clean, and showed the two brothers weren't afraid of hard work.

"No need to be skittish now, Jolie," Wes looked at her and smiled. "Jacy is going to be real pleased to meet you."

"She's a lady," Jolie managed to whisper. "She won't like me at all."

"You're a lady, too," Drew said confidently. "Jacy will love you."

"Drew's right. You'll be okay, Jolie," Wes reached over and patted her shoulder. "I know you didn't want to come here, but it will mean everything to Jacy, and I think someday soon you'll be happy we made you do it."

Drew gave her a wink, and then pointed. "Look there... Seems as though Jacy has already spotted us."

"Think I should ride ahead and prepare her?" Wes asked Drew's opinion.

"She already knows I'm here," Jolie told them matter-of-factly. "I can feel her, too." She urged her mount forward, suddenly anxious to meet her twin sister.

"Oh my God! Jolie!" were Jacy's first words as she ignored her husband and her brother-in-law to hug her long lost sister. "This is actually true!"

"It's true," Jolie laughed, hugging her back. "You could feel it yesterday, right?"

"Right," Jacy looked at her in awe. "Where have you been forever? Is our father still living?"

"No. He died over a year ago. Indians," Jolie explained.

"I'm sorry... I know you must have loved him, but he was a stranger to me," Jacy explained. "Mama is gone, too..."

"Wes told me. She was a good woman?"

"Yes... She wanted me to find you, and now you are here!" Jacy giggled. "I want you to stay."

"She's not going anywhere," Wes growled.

"Ohhhhhhhhhh! Wes!!!" Jacy threw herself at him and hugged him tightly, then kissed him. "I didn't see you!" she squealed. "Thank you for bringing Jolie to me. Thank you. Thank you. Thank you!" she punctuated her words with kisses.

Drew threw back his head and laughed at his brother's expression, then gave the horses over to one of the hired hands. "Come on inside, Jolie. Those two will be smooching for a while now," he predicted.

Jolie was impressed with the house, but felt very uncomfortable and out of place. She followed Drew into the kitchen, and relaxed a bit when he poured coffee for both of them.

"I learned some time ago it's best to be invisible when those two are like that," Drew grinned. "We won't see them until supper time." He placed the sugar bowl on the table so that Jolie could help herself.

"I can't believe you did that, you aggravating man!" Jacy's voice could be heard throughout the house. "Of all the nerve!" She burst into the kitchen, and stomped over to where Jolie stood, and then hugged her. "I'm sorry Wes was so mean to you! You must have thought he was crazy!"

"I did," Jolie immediately understood what Jacy was talking about, and a glance over her sister's shoulder at Wes's red face confirmed it.

"You had no right to assume something like that, Wesley Parker!" Jacy scolded, and then looked at Jolie, "What were you doing in a saloon?"

"Having a beer. It was hot outside..." Jolie explained.

"See...?" Wes pointed out. "See?"

"It doesn't matter! Even if I was to go into a saloon and order a beer, you wouldn't have the right to spank me for it!" Jacy sassed.

"The hell I wouldn't!" Wes argued.

"I wouldn't have it...! In front of all those men? How could you do such a thing, Wes? Especially when you thought it was ME?" Jacy was incensed.

Drew shook his head, and then whispered, "Jacy, you're walking on thin ice..."

"You stay out of this, Andrew Parker!" Jacy turned on him. "I can't believe you let him spank Jolie!"

"He spanked me, too!" Jolie was only too happy to tell on the man.

"WHAT?" Jacy screeched, and then rounded on her husband. "Wesley Parker... You are a no good skunk... and... No!!! Let me go!" Jacy's temper turned in another direction.

"I'm not going to have you railing at me the minute I get home, woman!" Wes scolded. "You asked me how I found Jolie, and I told you the truth of it, and you've been tearing a strip off me ever since. Now I'm going to remind you who wears the pants around here."

Jacy gasped as Wes sat down, and then pulled her over his lap. "No, Wes! Not in front of Drew and Jolie!"

"You yelled at me in front of them!" Wes pointed out, bringing his hand down on her skirt with a painful whap.

"Let her go!" Jolie jumped to her sister's defense.

Chapter Two

Jolie, this is between Wes and Jacy," Drew said firmly. "You aren't going to prevent it, so you might as well save yourself a tanning for interfering.

"You wouldn't!" Jolie looked at the big man in trepidation. He raised one dark eyebrow, and she swallowed hard. The meaning in his dark eyes was clear as could be. If she tried to save her sister from Wes, he was going to put her in the same position... and she couldn't bear the thought of another spanking.

Jacy kicked her legs, but Wes continued to swat her backside, in spite of her threats of dire consequences. "Are you ready to settle down, little wife, or do we need to take this upstairs and find your hairbrush?"

To Jolie's surprise, Jacy stopped fussing immediately. "I'll settle, Wes," Jacy said in a small voice.

"I thought you might," Wes grinned at her. "I thought you would want to spend your time talking to your sister rather than getting your butt paddled... but push me any further today, and you, me, and your hairbrush will have a long talk. Understand?" he asked with another hearty spank.

"Ouch! Yes, sir," Jacy replied, and then rubbed her smarting rear when Wes put her on her feet.

"Brother, we need to check on things around here, and give these two some time to talk," Wes said meaningfully.

Drew finished his coffee in one big gulp, and then got to his feet. He leaned over to whisper in Jolie's ear, "I'd better find you here when I get back, Miss Jolie, or I'll come after you..."

Jolie wanted to smack the overbearing jackass, but waited until the kitchen door closed behind them before giving vent to a muffled cry of outrage. "How do you stand them?" she asked her sister.

"It really isn't easy sometimes," Jacy continued to rub her stinging bottom. "I want to know everything about you, Jolie. Please say you'll stay and let us get acquainted..."

****

"Aren't you worried that Jolie will light out of here?" Drew asked his brother as he followed him to the corral.

"She's not going to leave... You're here..." Wes replied.

"What the hell does that mean?"

Wes looked at him, and then grinned. "Brother, that little girl is already in love with you. She's not going anywhere until she decides how she feels about that."

Drew felt his face turn red from the toes up. "How can you be so sure of that?"

"You aren't denying it, are you?"

****

"This soap smells like roses!" Jolie giggled as she enjoyed the luxury of a hot bath with real soap and towels.

"I make it myself," Jacy told her with a smile. "Roses are my favorite, too."

"Do you love Wes?" Jolie wanted to know.

"Yes, with all my heart."

"Even though he spanks you?"

"Even then. He only does it because he cares about me, Jolie. Mama really liked him, and she liked Drew, too." She poured another container of hot water into the tub… then asked, "What do you think of Drew?"

"I think he's a pain in the butt… quite literally!" she insisted, knowing full well her sister had seen the faint marks still left from the switch.

"I can't believe you had the nerve to shoot his hat! Why, the worst thing I've ever done was fill Wes's boots with molasses…!"

"You did!"

"Uh huh… The look on his face was priceless… Until I started laughing, and he realized it was me who did it, and not Drew…" She shook her head. "I didn't sit too well for a couple days."

"I'd like to get even with both of them for spanking me, and I think I know the perfect way," Jolie confided.

Jacy listened to her twin, and then smiled. "I know just the way to pull it off."

Jolie agreed to help, and made short work of finishing her bath. She toweled off, and was thrilled to don the clean under things and the dress her sister gave her. "This is the first dress I've worn since Pa's funeral," she admitted to her shocked sister. "Not much use for them on the trail."

"We'll get you some of your own real soon, Jolie, I promise,"Jacy declared, then bade her sister sit down while she brushed the tangles from the long blonde hair that was so much like her own. "Do you always wear your hair in a braid?" she asked.

"Easy to take care of," Jolie replied, then shrugged, "You can fix it however you like…"

Once Jacy was done, the two sisters stood side by side in front of the mirror, then giggled. "I wonder if Wes could tell us apart?" Jacy mused.

"I couldn't tell us apart if I didn't know…" Jolie decided.

They talked as they fixed supper and baked pies for dessert. "I feel as though I've known you forever, Jolie," Jacy said with a pleased smile. "I'm so happy you're here."

"I'm glad to be here," Jolie confessed, then surprised her sister with a spontaneous hug. "It's fun to have someone to share with…"

Jacy giggled, "They'll be in soon, and remember, we don't dare give ourselves away… Wes would spank for sure… and so would Drew."

****

"I hope that Jacy fixed something good to eat," Wes commented as he washed up at the pump on the back porch.

"And plenty of it," Drew added as he dried his face and hands on a clean towel. "But, she might have been too busy visiting with Jolie to even think about food, so don't go raisin' hell if she didn't cook… We can always fry up some ham and potatoes real quick like."

Wes frowned, but nodded. "Yea, okay. You're right. But I've missed her cooking," he added.

"Me too, brother. Little Jacy has us spoiled."

They stepped into the kitchen, and the two women turned and looked at them. Wes looked at Drew, and then chuckled. Without any hesitation, he walked over, and took Jacy in his arms and gave her a smacking kiss. "Something sure smells good, honey."

"You can tell us apart?" Jacy asked, disappointed.

"Yes, ma'am," Wes assured her.

"You look real pretty, Jolie," Drew complimented the other woman. "You and Jacy do look alike, but there is a difference," he added, taking a seat at the table. "Jacy, I don't know what's cooking, but I'm hungry, and it smells wonderful. You have Wes and me spoiled rotten."

"There's plenty to eat," Jacy assured them, her cheeks turning pink.

Jolie flashed her a warning glance, then helped to serve the stew. There were biscuits, too, and beets and eggs."

"This is great, honey," Wes finished his food.

"There's a pie for dessert," Jolie announced, then got up and cut huge pieces for both men. "Jacy?" she asked politely.

"No, not for me, Jolie. I'm full!" Jacy answered just the way they rehearsed.

"I know. I ate that second helping of stew... No room left for pie."

"I'll eat your piece then," Drew offered with a grin, happily indulging in the treat, and true to his word, he ate a second piece, which seemed to please Jolie to no end. "You must have baked this pie?" he smiled at her.

"I added a special ingredient," Jolie admitted, wondering how long it would be before the 'special ingredient' started working.

"Don't be too long cleaning up in here," Wes leaned down to whisper to Jacy. "I've missed my wife and intend to make an early night of it!"

"Wes!" Jacy was embarrassed, even though Drew just chuckled, and Jolie blushed and looked away.

Wes looked at Drew, and then said, "Do you have plans tonight, brother?"

"Going to hit the books, Wes. Want to record the business we did, and catch up on the ranch correspondence."

"Fair enough. While Jacy tidies in here, I'll go and check on that mare..."

"Jolie, if you're tired, there's no need for you to help with this. You can go on up to bed," Jacy told her sister.

"I'm not that tired," Jolie insisted, knowing full well that her sister was trying to get her safely tucked away before either of the men realized that they'd be spending most of the night trotting back and forth to the outhouse.

It wasn't long before Drew hurried through the kitchen and out the back door, and a few minutes later, Wes came inside and told his wife he wasn't feeling too well. The brothers took turns hurrying to the outhouse, and finally Drew realized that what was happening wasn't natural because neither of the women seemed to be having the same difficulty.

He spoke to Wes in the relative privacy of the study, and Wes shook his head in disbelief.

"Jacy wouldn't do that, Drew."

"Jolie would, and did. Remember her comment about 'special ingredients'?" Drew was sure of himself, and equally sure the little blonde was going to pay for making them so sick. But it would have to wait, he decided as he rushed from the house yet again.

"I didn't realize it would make them so sick," Jolie said, her blue eyes full of shame and remorse. "I used way too much..." She'd thrown the rest of the pie away right after supper so that no one else could possibly eat it by mistake. "I feel terrible, Jacy."

"Wes seems to be better now," Jacy felt so guilty. "His is finally wearing off..."

"Is there anything we could give Drew to make him feel better?"

"I'm not sure, but I can try," Jolie whispered, then put on a kettle of water to boil.

When Drew came back inside, he looked awful, and Jolie knew she had to apologize. "Drew... I'm sorry. I wanted to get even with you and Wes for spanking me, so I put something in the pie. I didn't know you'd get so sick, or I swear I wouldn't have done it."

Wes came into the kitchen as she was apologizing, and looked at Jacy, "Did you know Jolie was adding it to the pie, young lady?"

"Yes, sir," she replied truthfully.

"Then you'll share in the punishment," Wes decided.

"No, please...! Wes, it was all my idea... Not Jacy's..." Jolie wanted no part of getting her sister in trouble.

Jacy placed two cups of tea on the table, and then said, "This should help you both feel better. I'm sorry for my part in this. It was to be a little joke, but honestly, Jolie and I didn't mean for it to go so far."

Drew picked up the cup and sipped the bitter tea. If it helped to stop the horrible cramping, he would be grateful. "I don't think either Wes or I is up to discussing this tonight. I suggest you ladies get some sleep, and we'll talk in the morning."

Wes nodded, "Get on to bed. I'll stay up with Drew until he's feeling better."

Jacy didn't argue. She knew her husband well. She headed upstairs as fast as her two legs could take her, but Jolie stayed behind to argue with the man.

"Wes, please listen to me. Jacy isn't to blame... Just me..."

The angry redhead spun her around, and gave her backside a resounding whack. "To bed right now, young lady..."

****

Jolie threw herself on the bed and cried. Her sister must hate her. Her brother-in-law was angry with her. And Drew, well, he'd probably want her to leave just as soon as he could put her on a horse and say 'good riddance'. Why did she have to be so rotten at times? She was forever taking things just a step too far. She knew the ingredient worked, but why hadn't she thought to ask how much to use before going overboard...? And letting Drew eat a second piece of the pie was foolhardy. He was really ill, and it was all her fault.

Jolie couldn't stand it. She had to know how he was doing, and see for herself that he was recovering. She got up, and put the borrowed wrapper over the borrowed nightdress, and made her way downstairs. She could hear the men talking in the study, and she timidly knocked on the door.

Drew called out for her to enter, and Jolie did so. "I thought you were supposed to be in bed?" he scolded.

"I was worried about you," she confessed. "Are you any better?"

"I'm okay," he said, trying not to feel sympathetic towards her. It was obvious she'd been crying.

"I really am sorry," she insisted.

"You'll be even sorrier in the morning," Wes promised.

"Wes, I deserve whatever the two of you decide, but Jacy doesn't. It was all my idea. Honest. Please don't punish her."

"She knew about it, and she went along with it," Wes said. "She'll think twice the next time."

"Oh, please don't! She'll hate me!" Jolie begged tearfully. "I'll take her punishment, too...!"

"No you won't," Drew said in a rough tone of voice. "Wes will deal with his wife as he sees fit, and you, young lady, will be mine to punish." He gave her a moment to digest that fact, and then asked, "Just what do you think appropriate?"

"I don't know," Jolie admitted.

"What would your father have done?" Drew asked curiously.

"If I did it to him, he would have used his fists on me... to someone else, he wouldn't have cared... as long as he didn't suffer in any way from it."

"His fists?" Drew looked at her in alarm.

"My father wasn't a very nice man," Jolie confided. "The only thing that protected me from him was the fact that I got really good with a gun... and he knew I'd protect myself."

"So, you got away with anything and everything because you could outdraw your father?" Wes said in disbelief.

"He used his fists on her, little brother," Drew said softly. "I would have learned to defend myself, too."

"Yea... so would I..." Wes sighed. "Sounds like you and Jacy had similar backgrounds. Abby didn't discipline her either... even though she didn't hurt her..."

"I said I was sorry, and I really am," Jolie admitted. "Please don't take my behavior out on Jacy. I don't want her to hate me when I've just found her."

"She won't hate you, Jolie," Wes got to his feet and gave her a big, brotherly hug. "She knows she deserves a spankin', and she knows I'll tend to it in the mornin' first thing." He looked at Drew... "You're doin' okay now, so I'll go on up and get some sleep." He winked, then added, "Might be you'll want to take care of this young lady's guilt yet tonight?"

Drew smiled when Wes closed the door behind him. "Well, Miss Jolie, do you want to get this matter decided here and now?"

Jolie could feel her knees shaking, and her poor tummy was doing flip flops, but she nodded. Anything was better than worrying about what he intended to do to her in retaliation. "Just remember that I said I was sorry, and that I really, really do mean it!"

"What's fair, little girl?" Drew asked again. "Perhaps you should eat the rest of that pie?" he asked, knowing full well he'd never permit her to do so.

"I threw it away after supper," she admitted, her eyes wide.

"Good idea," he agreed. "Wes is going to take a hairbrush to Jacy, and I know for a fact he intends to do a thorough job of it. So, at the very least, you deserve a sound hiding. What else should I add to it? Perhaps a spanking for each time I had to trot outside?"

"No!" Jolie was appalled.

"Then you tell me what you deserve."

"Maybe chores?" she suggested.

"Could put you to mucking out stalls," Drew liked the idea. The smell alone this time of year was enough to knock a grown man over.

"Okay," Jolie immediately agreed. It was fair, and she was no stranger to hard work.

The first big difference between Jolie and Jacy, Drew discovered. Jolie would cry if Wes sent her to work in the barn. He needed something else... "You will also write an essay, telling what you did, and what you learned from the experience. Why it was not funny and why you deserve punishment. You will work on it in the evenings after you've worked in the barn all day, and you will work in the barn until the essay is finished to my satisfaction. I don't care if that takes a week. Understand?" Her eyes were full of disbelief, and he realized that writing the essay was something she didn't like at all.

"I'd rather take a whipping and have it over with," Jolie argued at once.

"Oh, never fear. You're going to get your butt spanked proper right here and now, little girl... And bright and early, you'll start mucking stalls. Tomorrow after supper, you'll sit at the kitchen table and work on your essay, and when it's finally done, you're going to get another whipping, and I'll decide after reading your essay just how hard and long it will be." He patted his thigh, then said, "Bring your bottom right here, Jolie, and let's see how red I can make it."

****

Wes closed the door quietly, but Jacy was instantly aware of his presence in the dark room. "Wes, I'm so sorry... Are you feeling better now?" she wanted to know, and he could hear the guilt in her voice.

"I'm fine, honey," he reassured her.

"What about Drew? Is he better, too?" There were actual tears in her voice.

"He's okay. Close your eyes and go to sleep," he whispered, undressing in the dark.

"I can't sleep," she admitted. "I feel too wretched."

"Need a spankin', huh?" he asked her.

"Yes, sir," Jacy admitted. "I'm sorry, Wes. Well and truly sorry, but I won't be able to forgive myself until I've been punished."

"I want you to think about what you did, wife. We'll discuss it in the morning, but you'll not get ease from the guilt until then," he decided.

Jacy tried one more time, "Please, Wes... Can't you spank me right now?"

"I could, but I said that you would have to wait until morning. Ask me again, and you'll suffer the guilt until bedtime tomorrow." His voice was gruff, but his arms were tender as he pulled her warm body close to him. "Now close your eyes and go to sleep."

****

Jolie swallowed nervously, but decided she'd earned a spanking, and she would take it without a fuss. She walked over to Drew's chair, and placed herself over his lap.

"Pull up the gowns, Jolie. I won't spank you on top of clothing. Would lose its effect."

Jolie was embarrassed, but reminded herself that he'd already seen her bare. At least this time she was face down, and he couldn't see her feminine parts... She pulled the gown and robe up to the top of her hips, and blushed when his hand patted her familiarly. "You still have traces of the switching I gave you..."

"I know... It's still uncomfortable when I sit."

"It's going to be even more uncomfortable now. I have no intention of sparing you, young lady. What you did was not funny. It was dangerous." He punctuated his words with a slap to her right cheek. "Do you agree?"

"Yes..."

"Yes what?"

Jolie closed her eyes, but said, "Yes, sir."

"That's much better. I'm going to spank you hard, Jolie, and you will take it because it is deserved. You will report to the table at five am sharp, and be prepared to put in a long, hard day in the barn cleaning out stalls. After supper, you will get paper, pen and ink, and sit at the kitchen table and work on your essay until bedtime. If you don't finish the essay tomorrow evening, then you will spend another day in the barn, and complete the essay in the evening. If I read it, and it's not acceptable, you'll be spanked again, and you will start over. If I do accept what you write, then you'll get your whipping, and this will all be forgiven. Is this all understood?" he asked.

"I don't write very well, Drew. I didn't get to school much," Jolie admitted.

"I'll take that into account," he answered, then felt her muscles relax. He was right. She was dreading the essay more than the spankings, or the work in the stables. "This, little girl, is what I think of your prank..."

Jolie gasped as his hard hand landed on her right cheek. He continued to spank one spot until it was on fire, then moved to the left cheek and proceeded to do the same there. Over and over, his hand fell, covering every inch of her bottom, her thighs, and her sit spot. And still he spanked her. Jolie couldn't help crying as the pain intensified, and she wondered how on earth she would manage to sit at all the next day.

Drew could feel the heat coming off her backside, and was pretty sure that she was feeling each and every swat. Her butt and her thighs were a deep crimson, and he decided she'd had enough. He pulled the gown down, and then helped her up. "I suggest you get a few hours of sleep, Jolie. Tomorrow is going to be a long day for you."

Jolie took herself off to bed, and cried herself to sleep. She couldn't believe how much her life had changed in such a short period of time.

Drew banged on her door while it was still dark outside. "You have fifteen minutes to be downstairs and at the table," he told her. "If you're late, we'll start the day with another tanning."

Jolie was too sore to contemplate another spanking. She slipped into her pants and shirt, and quickly braided her hair. It would be easier to muck stalls dressed like a boy. She hurried downstairs and entered the kitchen just as Drew was grabbing a piece of kindling from the box to come after her. He looked at her pointedly, and then dropped it back into the box. "One more minute would have been too late," he warned.

He poured a cup of coffee for them both, and then said, "We'll break in about three hours to eat some breakfast. Drink up, and let's get to work."

Jolie was no stranger to a pitchfork, and she was a hard worker. Drew was impressed with the real effort she put into the job, and instead of having to scold and threaten her with a strapping to get some work out of her, she made it look easy.

"You've done this before," he said conversationally as he came up behind her.

"I had to earn money somehow," she shrugged. "It's honest work."

"I'm not so sure it's a punishment, though," he stated.

She leaned on the fork handle and said, "I feel punished each and every time I try to sit down. My sit upon is really sore... and the worst part is knowing that my sister is going to get spanked for something I started and did. I wish you would talk to Wes, and ask him not to punish Jacy. I'll do anything..." she offered.

Drew immediately realized she didn't have a clue what most women meant when they said that. "You just keep working, and let Miss Jacy suffer her own consequences. She earned a good spanking, and I'll trust Wes to see that she gets one."

****

Jacy opened her blue eyes, and then bit her lower lip. Wes was already awake, and he was sitting on a wooden chair they kept in their bedroom for one purpose only... It was the chair he sat on when he spanked her. It was morning, and time for her to pay for her foolishness of the day before.

Wes didn't say a word. He didn't have to. Jacy knew exactly what was expected of her. It was embarrassing for her, but it was a ritual they'd established, and it worked well. He watched as she used the porcelain chamber pot she kept pushed under the bed. Once she was finished relieving herself, she went to the corner, and pulled up her gown to expose her bottom. She had no idea how long she would have to stand there. It could be only a few seconds, or he might let her stand there for an hour or longer. Part of the punishment was in not knowing what to expect.

Wes decided he would be merciful, and make the corner time short. "You can come over here, Jacy," he called to her, and Jacy came at once. Her blue eyes were filled with tears of remorse. "Why are you going to be spanked this morning?" he asked, wanting to be sure she knew exactly why she was going to get a sound paddling.

"Because I went along with Jolie's prank... because it wasn't funny... because you and Drew were ill... and because it could have been much worse. I'm ashamed of myself, honey," she added contritely.

"Is there any thing else I should know...? Any reason at all this spanking shouldn't take place?"

"No, sir," Jacy replied, then said in a small voice, laced with guilt. "I deserve a spanking."

"Yes, you do." He didn't believe in mincing words. He took her arm and helped her across his knee, then waited patiently while she tugged her gown up past her waist. He always made her bare herself for punishments to prove to him that she accepted his right to administer correction when it was necessary. Today there would be no warm up. Just the hairbrush, and all out from the start to the finish. Jacy wouldn't forget this spanking any time soon.

Jacy hollered from the first splat of the hairbrush on her tender skin. It hurt, and Wes wasn't going easy on her this time. She wiggled and squirmed, and he finally stopped long enough to pin her legs between his, and pin her arm to her back. She was helpless to protect herself, and was sobbing hoarsely before he ended the punishment. He sent her to the corner when he was done, and Jacy knew it was time to pull herself together. Wes would question her in a few minutes, and if her answers were not to his liking, she would find herself over the bed, receiving licks from his belt.

Wes gave her a full fifteen minutes, and then called her over. "What do you have to say for yourself, Jacy? Have you learned anything?"

"I'm truly sorry, Wes," she said again. "I won't ever do anything like that again."

"Is that the best you can do?" he demanded, obviously not appeased.

"I don't know what else to say," Jacy cried.

"Over the bed, and I'll give you something more to help you think."

"No, please! I'm sorry!" Jacy insisted.

"That 'no' will cost you ten extra. Want a few more?"

"No, sir! I'm sorry!" Jacy hurried over to the bed, and knelt there, sticking her bottom up in the air. The first lick of the belt caught her sit spot, and she cried out. Nine more followed, and she was sobbing and struggling to maintain her position."

"Have you thought of anything else?" Wes asked.

"Yes, sir. I will apologize to Drew," she promised.

"That's good. Anything else?"

"I won't ever do it again. It wasn't funny, and it was a dangerous thing to do."

"Much better."

"Please, Wes... I am so sorry. Please forgive me?"

"You're forgiven," he said softly, touching her back and rubbing gently. "We have a few extras to take care of, though," he said with genuine regret in his voice. "I'll give you a choice... Ten extra licks on your thighs, or ten minutes chewing soap for the 'no'?"

Jacy couldn't help crying. She hated and despised soap, and it was the way Wes taught her to control her bad mouth. She also hated having her thighs strapped, and they were already so sore. She knew better than hesitate much longer, though, or Wes could decide to do both. "Please, I'll take the extras, honey. I'm sorry, though," she added, hoping he would be merciful, but knowing he wouldn't be. Extras were always harder than the others…

Wes nodded, and then said, "I'll hold you, sweetheart, and get it over with fast." True to his word, his hand went around and under her waist to keep her steady, and he gave her the ten in rapid succession. When it was over, he dropped the belt, then held her close and let her cry, soothing her with words of love and forgiveness.

When she settled, he asked, "Would you like to go back to bed…? I can fix breakfast this morning…"

"I'll do it, honey," she tried to smile. "It'll help to take my mind off rubbing…"

"Rubbing will just earn you another spanking," he warned, "and I really would hate to have to do that right now. Your backside is a real mess."

"I won't rub," she promised.

Wes gave her a gentle kiss then headed downstairs. He was going to find his brother, and make damned sure that Miss Jolie was sporting an equally sore backside.

****

Jolie hated the thought of going inside for breakfast when Drew told her it was time to eat. She wasn't ready to face her sister or Wes. "I'm not hungry," she told Drew, continuing to work.

"Then you will come and sit at the table anyway. Part of your punishment is sitting on that butt, young lady," Drew didn't give her a choice in the matter.

Jolie reluctantly put the fork aside, removed her gloves, and then followed Drew to the house. She washed up at the pump, and blushed when her stomach rumbled. Drew smiled knowingly, and then leaned down to whisper, "You have to face them sometime, kid." He held open the door, and Jolie reluctantly entered.

"Take a seat, Jolie," Wes pointed her toward a chair, and Jolie promptly folded a leg under her in an attempt to keep her backside off the chair.

"Sit properly, Jolie," Drew scolded her, and stood there until her backside and thighs were flush against the chair.

"You can sit, too, Jacy," Wes said, realizing his wife was puttering to keep from taking her seat.

"I'm sorry, Jacy," Jolie whispered contritely as her sister eased herself on her chair.

"Looks like you got into just as much trouble as I did," Jacy smiled fondly.

"Even more," Drew replied, and went on to tell how the little blonde was making amends.

"That is too much, Drew!" Jacy protested, and one look from Wes was all it took to quiet her.

"It was Jolie's idea, and it has consequences, Jacy," Drew said gently. "Eat hearty, Jolie; you have a lot of stalls left."

The sisters ate quickly, but the brothers seemed to enjoy taking their time, and neither lady was allowed to get up until they were finished eating. "Jacy, you have something to say to Drew...?" Wes prompted.

"Yes, I do," Jacy agreed without hesitation. "Drew, I am terribly sorry for last night. It wasn't funny, and I give you my word it will never happen again. Wes said I am to ask you for additional consequences..." she was embarrassed.

Drew gave his younger brother a look, then decided that perhaps it was a good thing to let little Jacy know that he expected better of her. "Very well, Jacy, you are confined to the kitchen today. These are the only chairs you are to sit on. Is this acceptable to you, Wes?"

"Yes, it is," Wes agreed. Trust his brother to come up with something that Jacy would hate, but that wouldn't inflict any more pain on her poor backside. "Jacy, you heard Drew. I expect you to obey him. You are confined to the kitchen, except for the chores you have outside."

"Yes, sir."

Jolie wanted to die. Would Drew expect her to ask for consequences from the tall redhead, too? Nothing more was said, and soon she was back in the barn, working hard. At noon, she had to deal with sitting on the chair again, and by the end of the day, she was done mucking out all the stalls.

"You did a good job, Jolie," Drew was full of praise for her. He hadn't caught her shirking even once today, and in good conscience, felt she'd earned the right to do as she pleased tomorrow, even if she wasn't able to get the essay done tonight.

They ate supper, and Drew didn't argue when she offered to help Jacy with the dishes. He knew she was stalling, and he was letting her get away with it. He further shocked her by suggesting she take a nice bath, and then come to him in the study for paper and a pen and ink. The smile Jolie gave him was worth the teasing Wes gave him.

"Miss Jacy," he addressed his sister-in-law when Jolie went upstairs, "Have you stayed in the kitchen today?"

"Yes," her lower lip trembled, and Drew felt guilty. "Was I too hard on you, hon?" he asked softly.

"No... I'm sorry, Drew," she acknowledged. "I promise it won't ever happen again."

"I know it won't, honey," he got up and gave her an affectionate hug. "You go on and do as you please now. I think you've been punished enough for this mistake."

Jacy didn't need to be told twice. She really wanted to ask that Jolie be let off too, but knew that it would cost her another spanking from her husband if she did. He'd made that perfectly clear earlier. She found Jolie, and spent an hour with her while she bathed, and freshened up. They giggled and cried, and once Jacy learned that Jolie didn't regard the barn work as anything dreadful, Jacy relaxed a bit. She offered to help with the essay, but Jolie politely refused.

"I owe it to Drew to do it myself," she explained. "The worst part will be sitting there while I write it," she admitted. "I kind of know already what I want to say."

"I can't believe he's going to punish you again after you write it!" Jacy was shocked and dismayed.

Chapter Three

Jolie was all by herself in the kitchen, and she couldn't concentrate. Sitting on the chair was proving impossible, and she wanted nothing more than to charge into the other room, and simply refuse to write the essay. After all, what was the worst that could happen? She was on her feet and through the door before she could give it another thought.

"I don't want to write an essay!" she announced at the doorway of the parlor.

Jacy closed her eyes... Wes grinned and looked at his brother. Drew closed the book he was reading and came and took her arm and marched her into the kitchen.

"I thought we decided last night that writing this essay would be a part of your punishment."

"It's too hard," Jolie insisted. "I can't concentrate while sitting here."

"Butt hurt too much?" Drew guessed.

"I'm really sore," Jolie admitted, then said, "but it's more than that. I can't get it right. I know what I want to say, but I can't spell half the words, and I keep making mistakes..." She pointed at the pile of rolled up balls of paper.

Drew picked up one after another and smoothed them out, then tried reading. Finally, he looked at her, and saw her chin jut out stubbornly. "If you were writing, what would you say?"

Jolie shrugged, then told him, praying that he would be satisfied with an oral essay. She talked for a while, and was relieved when he smiled at her.

"You spent a lot of time thinking about this today, didn't you?" he wanted to know.

"Yes, I did… but I can't get it down on paper…" her blue eyes filled with tears of frustration.

"It's okay. I'm going to let you off this time, in exchange for something else."

"What?" she asked, afraid it was going to mean another spanking on top of the one she still faced.

"I want you to spend some time with Jacy each day, learning to write and spell better. Would you be willing to do that, Jolie?"

"Yes, providing she doesn't mind teaching me."

"She won't mind at all," he assured her. "It was a good essay you thought out," he complimented her.

"Thank you." She dreaded what was going to happen next. He was going to give her another whipping, and she was afraid it would be as bad as the switching he gave her.

"I'd say you learned your lesson well, wouldn't you?"

"Yes, sir," she replied honestly.

"Am I ever going to have to worry about you doing that again?"

"No, sir. I promise I won't."

Drew pulled her up off the chair and gave her a hug. "Do you want to finish this off tonight? Or wait until tomorrow?"

"I want it done," Jolie declared.

"Okay, pull up your skirts, and bend over the table." He removed his belt. "Wes told me he gave Jacy ten with his belt on top of the spanking she got with her hairbrush. She also got ten extra for not getting into position. You're in position, and if you stay there on your own, there won't be any extra for you to worry over, but I'm going to give you fifteen since you were more responsible than Jacy was. You can cry, but you will stay in position, or face extra..."

Jolie was embarrassed, and terrified that Wes or Jacy would come into the kitchen and see her like this. She simply wanted Drew to get it over with. He gave her the first lick over her sore cheeks, and the second followed right below. The next two were on her thighs, and then he spanked her cheeks again and again. The last five fell on her sit spot, and then it was all over. Jolie wanted nothing more than to run to her room and cry, but Drew had other ideas. He pulled her close and hugged her tightly.

Jolie felt safe in his arms, and when he lowered his mouth to hers and kissed her gently, she found herself returning his kiss, and wanting even more.

"I would like for us to see where this can go, Jolie," Drew said when he released her. "I felt an attraction to you when I first saw you. I think you might feel the same...?"

"I have to ask you something, Drew..." It pained her, but she had to know... "Do you want me for me, or because you can't have Jacy?"

He reached out and gently caressed her cheek. "I love Jacy as a sister," he admitted. "What I feel for you is not the least bit brotherly."

Jolie smiled in relief, then said, "I would like to get to know you better, too, Drew."

****

"Now, sweetie, don't cry," Wes consoled Jacy as best he could. He'd had to physically restrain her to keep her from rushing into the kitchen when Jolie cried out in pain.

"I should have stopped her..." Jacy cried. "I hate it that Drew is still punishing her... She had to clean stalls all day, and that is really hard work."

"Yes, it is," Wes agreed.

"Please, honey... Talk to him... Remind him that Jolie is new here... and ..."

"You're about to cross a line, little lady," Wes warned her, putting his finger on her sweet lips. "Maybe we ought to go on up to bed and leave them to settle their differences?"

"It's really early!" Jacy complained.

"And I've been gone a long time, and had my homecoming ruined last night," Wes pouted deliberately in an attempt to get a smile. It worked. Jacy blushed a pretty pink. "If you're too sore, sweetie, I won't insist," he said with consideration.

Jacy kissed him full on the lips, then whispered in a seductive tone of voice, "I would very much like to go to bed early, Mr. Parker..."

****

Jolie and Jacy were inseparable, and Drew and Wes had no reason to complain. The meals they cooked were always delicious, and the sisters seemed to delight in making them feel special. Jolie went for long walks with Drew in the evening, and he told Wes that he was thinking of asking her to marry him.

Jacy was teaching Jolie to spell, and to write, and Jolie was teaching her sister things that Wes wasn't too thrilled to have his wife learning... such as using a gun. The first time he'd heard shots, he'd raced to the back of the house to see Jacy shooting at empty tin cans she'd placed on a fence. They'd argued, but in the end, Drew had convinced him that it couldn't hurt for Jacy to know how to use a gun. There were times when she was all by herself at the house when they were out working on the range, and the hands were elsewhere.

The only drawback to the whole situation was Jolie's attitude about going into town. She didn't want to, and nothing Jacy said could convince her to change her mind. She would get that stubborn tilt to her chin, and flat out refuse each and every time she was asked to go along.

Finally, Drew decided it was time to intervene. "Do you have a wanted poster out on you, kid?" he asked with a wide grin.

"Of course not!" Jolie answered.

"Then why don't you want to go," he asked seriously.

"Doesn't matter why not. I'm just not going to go."

"You're upsetting Jacy," he told her.

"Only because she doesn't understand," Jolie pouted.

"Jolie, I've had enough of this. We're going into town tomorrow, and you're going with us."

"No I'm not!" she argued, and within seconds found herself looking at the carpet in the parlor. "No!" she cried out.

Drew spanked her bottom three times, and then asked, "Are you ready to change your mind, little girl".

Jolie really did NOT want a spanking. Her bottom was all better now and she wanted to keep it that way. She would simply have to go into town and hope for the very best. "I'll go," she conceded, and to her relief, Drew righted her and sat her on his lap.

"Want to tell me why you're so worried?" he asked again, but didn't persist when Jolie shook her head 'no'. He just pulled her close and gave her a kiss that curled her toes and made her long for more than just kisses.

****

"I expect you to take care of the matter as soon as we get to town, Jacy," Wes was in a stubborn mood. "Do you understand?"

Jacy's face turned pink, and Jolie sensed her sister was struggling to keep a tight rein on her temper. Jacy gave her husband a look, but spoke quietly, "I understand, Wes."

"Fine. I'll drop you off at the Church, and you can walk over to the Mercantile and meet Jolie there afterwards. Drew and I need to take care of some business at the bank, and once we're through there, we'll meet up with you and go and have something to eat."

"Jolie, you are to do some shopping while we're in town. We're not so poor that we can't afford some new dresses for you," Drew said with a smile, hoping she wouldn't be offended.

"I wear pants," Jolie told him flatly, even though she'd donned a riding skirt of her sister's for the trip into town. Jacy had warned her that neither of the men would let her off the ranch wearing pants, and Jolie had given in mostly to keep from embarrassing Jacy.

"You wear pants because that's all you have. Buy some dresses, or I'll buy them for you," Drew said sternly. Jolie's chin turned up, and he realized that the little blonde had no intention of doing as he said. "If you don't pick out something for yourself by the time I get to the Mercantile, little girl, I'll try out one of Ed's hairbrushes on your backside!" That earned him a heated look, but Wes pulled the wagon in front of the minister's house at that moment, and Drew held his tongue.

"Remember our discussion, Jacy," Wes warned as Jacy jumped down, then he slapped the reins on the horses' rumps and headed for the Mercantile. "Jolie, you're Jacy's sister, and that makes you family. You enjoy doing a bit of shopping now,"

Wes added his voice to Drew's, and smiled as she ignored Drew's hand and jumped down on her own.

Drew shook his head as she stomped into the store. "She's looking for a tanned butt, little brother."

"Maybe Jacy will convince her to be reasonable," Wes said hopefully.

"Don't you think maybe you should have gone with Jacy to take care of that apology?" Drew looked at Wes.

"Didn't dare," the redhead admitted with a grin. "That woman makes me as mad as she does Jacy, and I'd do more than call her a 'mean old witch'. Jacy will apologize, and that'll be the end of it."

Drew privately thought that Wes was just asking for trouble, but what did he know?

****

Jolie pretended an interest in some items on a table outside the front door of the Mercantile while she waited for Wes and Drew to head around the corner, and out of sight. Then she turned on her heel and ran lightly to the spot where her sister was waiting impatiently. "Okay, let's get this over with."

"I just can't apologize, Jolie," Jacy insisted. "The woman is a mean old witch, and why should I say I'm sorry when I'm not?"

"To keep Wes from taking a switch to you?" Jolie said matter-of-factly.

"It's just not fair, Jolie," Jacy insisted, but she led the way to the front door of the parsonage, and knocked.

Jolie just hoped the woman was gracious. She wasn't sure how she would control HER temper if the old biddy was mean to Jacy.

"Oh, it's you!" the gray haired woman's smile faded abruptly.

"Mrs. Fellows, I came to apologize for calling you a mean old witch," Jacy said in a small voice.

"I don't believe you for one second," the woman said astutely. "I've half a mind to speak to Jacob and have him denounce you at Sunday's services," she threatened.

"I wouldn't if I were you," Jolie declared.

"You... Oh my God... Satan's children!" the woman backed away, looking from one to the other.

"That's right, and I'll put a curse on you if you ever speak hatefully to my sister again, you mean old witch!" Jolie threatened the woman, then gave her what she hoped was a purely evil smile. She raised both hands, wiggled her fingers, and then said a few words of Apache she'd managed to pick up.

Lucy Fellows let out a scream, and promptly fainted.

Jolie and Jacy looked at each other, and then started giggling. They heard commotion from inside the house, and decided to make their escape while they could.

****

Wes grinned at his brother, "I'm sure that Jolie is doing what she was told, big brother. I don't think she was too excited at the prospect of trying out one of Ed's hairbrushes.

"I wish I hadn't promised to do that, Wes," Drew told him. "Jolie's got a lot of pride, and I know things haven't been easy for her... She's not used to letting anyone do things for her."

"We're family, though," Wes argued. "Don't you worry; I'll bet Jacy has her picking out fabric right now."

"We'll see," Drew was skeptical. But, to his surprise, the sisters were doing just that when he and Wes walked into the store. He walked over to see how they were doing, and was pleased to see Jolie's eyes sparkling in good humor. "That one is pretty," he pointed to the one she was looking at."

"I like it, too," Jolie admitted shyly. "But, I've already let Jacy talk me into two other pieces." Her eyes were wistful, but her pride was telling her 'no'.

"I'd like for you to have this one, too, Jolie, and I promise I won't say another word about buying any more until these are done up."

Jolie glanced at her sister, and didn't have much trouble reading her expression. They'd agreed that placating and humoring the two men would get them out of town faster, and perhaps keep their husbands from learning what happened at the preacher's house. "Okay, Drew. Thank you for being so generous."

Drew was pleased, and satisfied he was making some progress with the feisty Jolie. All it took was a firm hand and some gentle praise, and she would come around in no time at all.

Wes leaned down and whispered quietly, "Did you apologize, Jacy?"

"Yes, Wes," Jacy replied, her cheeks turning a guilty pink, but Wes just attributed that to embarrassment.

"Good girl," he kissed the top of her head. "Did you pick anything new for yourself?"

"I don't need anything," she insisted with a smile. "You're always buying me presents."

"Maybe a new hat?"

"Maybe some raisins?" she asked hopefully. "They are pretty expensive, though," she warned. "I'd like to bake a pie...?"

"Raisin pie sounds tasty," Wes agreed. "You just get what you need, honey."

They quickly finished up their shopping, and Drew suggested they eat in the small restaurant across the street.

****

"Wonder what the heck is goin' on?" Wes grumbled. "Folks aren't usually so darn rude!"

"I've had just about enough of it," Drew commented. "They're acting like they've never seen a set of twins before!"

Jolie quickly picked up her coffee cup and took a sip, glancing at her sister over the rim. Jacy was blushing again, and if she didn't stop, they were going to be in serious trouble. "I'm getting a headache," she suddenly announced. "Can we go home now, Wes?"

"Sure." Wes was all concern for his wife, and Drew hurriedly paid the bill.

They were just to the door when it suddenly opened, the tiny bell jingling furiously. "There you are!" Pastor Fellows' voice bellowed across the room. "How dare you come to my home and cast your evil spells on my Lucy? She is overwrought... and convinced she will never walk again!"

"Oh, don't be silly," Jolie scoffed. "All I did was wiggle my fingers at her and say 'hello' in Apache!"

"You cursed her, and she cannot walk!"

"Jolie did not curse her!" Jacy argued. "She defended me. Your wife is not a nice person, Pastor Fellows! She is mean and hateful, and she is a mean old witch, and I'm not one bit sorry for calling her one!"

"Young woman, she is crippled and cannot walk. I want you to remove the spell at once," the blustering man demanded.

"Pastor, the only thing these young ladies are guilty of is bad manners. They do not have special powers. I suggest you tell your wife to stop acting like a hysterical fool and get her butt out of bed." Wes joined in the fray.

"Jolie, you are going to go and apologize to Mrs. Fellows right this minute," Drew said in a firm voice.

Drew took Jolie's arm and marched her to the parsonage; Wes and Jacy following with the wagon. Pastor Fellows opened the front door, and led them through the house and into a bedroom, where Lucy Fellows lay moaning. Jolie looked at Jacy and rolled her eyes. There were at least three women fussing over Lucy, and Lucy was making the most of it.

"How could you do such a wicked, evil thing to our dear Lucy?" Abigail Winters asked tearfully.

"I didn't do anything to her," Jolie replied calmly. "She was being mean to my sister..."

"Evil, that's what the two of you are. You belong to Satan!" Lucy screeched dramatically.

"Jolie, apologize immediately, and take back whatever you said," Drew gave her arm a meaningful shake.

"I apologize for wiggling my fingers like this," Jolie demonstrated, "and I apologize for wishing you a good day in Apache." Jolie couldn't help smiling when the woman's face turned purple with suppressed fury.

"How dare you come in here and mock me? I can't walk! Pastor, make them leave... I don't want this evil in my home... You must denounce them from the pulpit... Arrrrrrrrrrrrrrggggggggggghhhhhhhhhhhh!" Lucy let out a scream when Wes picked up the pitcher of cold water from the stand and dumped it below her waist. In the next minute, she was standing beside the bed, glaring at him angrily. "You got my mattress all wet! You horrible man!"

"It's a miracle! You can walk again," Wes said solemnly.

Lucy's face turned even redder as she realized she was standing in mixed company, wearing nothing but a nightdress, which was soaked clear through.

"Lucy," Pastor Fellow's voice boomed into every corner of the room. "You were pretending!" he accused. "You lied to all of us about being cursed... "

"Pastor... You don't understand... They look alike, and that is truly evil...!" Lucy's lower lip trembled. "You must denounce them..."

"You lied, and scared me half to death with this nonsense of curses... and I won't have it." He turned to Jacy, "Mrs. Parker, I would like to hear what happened last week from your point of view." He listened attentively while Jacy explained, even when she admitted to calling the older woman a mean old witch, and when she added that she came here to apologize at Wesley's bidding.

"Woman, I've suspected for some time that you weren't the innocent victim in all these situations, and it appears I'm right. I think your behavior warrants punishment. You may go to that corner and kneel until I am ready to strap you."

"No... Pastor... Not with everyone here!" she whispered, her face crimson.

"I did not ask you to raise your gown, but I will do so if you do not obey me instantly."

Lucy moved into the corner, and knelt there, sobbing.

"I will apologize for my wife's behavior until she is willing to do so for herself," Pastor Fellows spoke to Jacy and Jolie.

"Jacy and Jolie aren't completely innocent in all this, either, Pastor," Drew spoke up, and Jolie could see he wasn't the least bit happy with her. "I know that my fiancée is going to answer for her rude behavior," and a glance at Wes had him adding, "And Wes will be dealing with Jacy."

"I'm sure you know what is best," Pastor smiled in understanding. He showed them to the door, and all too soon the foursome was on their way home.

Jacy kept glancing at Wes, then at Jolie, and Jolie could see her twin was worried. "I don't know why you two are so upset with us...?" she declared. "The Pastor's wife is not a very nice woman. Jacy apologized to her, and she refused to accept it, and she threatened Jacy. You couldn't expect me to let her get away with that, now could you?"

"You weren't even supposed to be there, Jolie," Drew looked down at her. "And pretending to put a curse on the woman...! You will never pull another stunt like that!"

"Oh, come on...!" Jolie scolded. "Wes, admit it, you thought it was funny, too."

"I think that two little girls need their bottoms switched," Wes answered, then pulled on the reins and stopped the horses. "And I think that tree right there has plenty of nice switches on it." He jumped down off the wagon, and lifted Jacy down. Wes handed her his knife, then gave her a smart slap on her bottom. "Go and cut a switch, Jacy, and peel it."

Jolie was so busy watching in dismay that she didn't realize Drew had dismounted until he grabbed her around the waist and lifted her down. "You, little girl, can do the same." Jolie stared at the knife in her hand, and looked up at him. The expression in his dark eyes was daring her to argue, and Jolie knew from experience that she was going to get switched, no matter what. Reluctantly, she went to join her twin.

Jacy had already found one that was about as thick as her middle finger at the base, and she was stripping the bark and leaves from it, leaving it green... and very pliable. When Jolie started to cut one, Jacy shook her head 'no'. "Too thin," she whispered. "Drew will wear it out fast, and then make you cut another... This one," she pointed to another that was about the same size as hers.

Jolie quickly cut it off, and then started preparing it the way her sister was. It was ready all too soon, and the girls looked at each other in trepidation. "I'm sorry I got you into trouble, Jolie," Jacy whispered. "Lucy Fellows is an old witch!!"

"We'll fix her," Jolie promised, already planning to get even with the woman at the earliest possibility.

"Stalling is goin' to cost you a few more stripes, Jacy. Get over here," Wes called impatiently.

Jacy and Jolie hurried over to the wagon, and Wes took Jacy's arm and pulled her around to the other side.

"Take off that skirt," Drew told Jolie, and she heard Wes ordering Jacy to do the same. Jolie knew it wouldn't do any good to plead. She handed the switch to Drew, and undid the skirt and laid it over the side of the wagon. "Drop your drawers to your ankles."

Jacy was embarrassed for her sister, and not a bit surprised when Wes gave her the same order. The brothers had obviously planned this... and she wouldn't be surprised if they'd agreed on how many to deliver to each bottom! "How many, Wes?" she asked fearfully. She could stand ten or twelve, but please... no more than that...

"You're gettin' twenty-five to start with, and another twenty-five when I get you home."

"Wes, no!!!!! That's too much!" Jacy protested.

"Drew?" Jolie looked at him in horror. "You aren't...? That woman is responsible for all of this, and she deserved it..."

"First of all, little girl, this matter was between Wes and Jacy. You had no call to stick your nose in. You tried to scare Lucy Fellows on purpose. You were just as rude as she was, and I won't tolerate this type of behavior. You're getting the same as Jacy," he told her sternly. "Now turn around, put your hands on the wheel, and stick your fanny out here for a good switching. If you let go of the wheel, or twist away, I'll add five extra each time."

"You heard Drew, Jacy. Hands on the wheel. You're not going to sit comfortable for a while. I expect my wife to behave, no matter how any one else acts... You are not to call people names, and if I tell you to apologize, you do it properly."

Jolie felt the first line of fire across her bottom and gasped. This was worse than she thought it would be. Within a few seconds, her bottom felt as though a swarm of bees were stinging her over and over... and then Drew started on her thighs. She couldn't help screaming in pain. The switching seemed to go on and on and on, but somehow she managed to hold onto the wheel and not earn any extras. The last couple were the worst; they landed right where she had to sit, and the sting was unbearable. Jolie was sobbing by the time Drew told her to pull up her drawers, and put her skirt on. Her fingers were shaking badly, but she managed to do as she was told.

Jacy wasn't as lucky as Jolie. She let go of the wheel twice to reach back and try to protect her backside from the switch, earning herself another ten on top of the twenty-five. Wes took his time delivering them, and scolding her, and then had to help her get dressed. He plunked her on the wagon seat with orders to sit still.

Drew helped Jolie climb up, and noticed that she wasn't sitting too well either. "That sore butt will give you something to think about the rest of the way home." He handed her the switch. "Twenty-five more, and I expect you to ready yourself the minute we get home."

The ride home was miserable, and Jacy and Jolie sniffled all the way. Sitting still was hard to do, but Wes growled each and every time one of them wiggled. Jolie was both relieved and apprehensive when the ranch came into sight. She wanted off the wagon seat, but she didn't want another switching on top of the one she'd had. Surely Drew and Wes wouldn't be mean enough to whip them again...?

"You two can get inside," Wes ordered as he helped Jacy, then Jolie, down from the wagon.

"I should start supper, honey," Jacy said tentatively, looking up at Wes for approval.

"Go ahead," he agreed. "It's going to take Drew and me a good while to unload this wagon.

Jacy nodded, and then hurried in to the kitchen. "Maybe if we fix something really good to eat, they'll forget about finishing our punishment," she whispered to Jolie.

Jolie prayed that was true as she started peeling potatoes.

****

"Wes, I don't think either of those girls needs another switching," Drew said without preamble as they carried bags of feed into the barn. "After all, they were rude to a woman who baited them… They didn't risk their lives…"

"I know," Wes grumbled. "That's why I set Jacy to fixing supper. Poor kid could barely sit on the wagon seat." He dropped the bag of feed beside the one Drew put down. "Let's let them squirm until after supper, then we can accept their promises to be good," he suggested with a grin.

Drew chuckled, and then worked with his younger brother to empty the wagon.

****

"Supper was real good, honey," Wes commented.

"Thank you," Jacy smiled, trying her best not to squirm on the chair. Sitting through supper had been difficult.

"Jolie, you're awful quiet," Drew looked at the little blonde. She'd pushed her food around on her plate, but had eaten very little. "Still hurting?" he asked.

Jolie nodded, "Please don't whip us again," she pleaded. "We're sorry we embarrassed you today."

"Are you sorry, too, Jacy?" Wes asked directly.

"Yes, I am. I promise to control my tongue in the future," Jacy was sincere.

"I believe they are sincere, Drew... What do you think?" Wes turned to his brother.

"I think we should give them another chance, Wes. After all, Lucy Fellows was guilty, too..."

Jolie and Jacy couldn't believe what they were hearing, but they weren't about to question their good fortune. They each thanked the brothers, then hurried to clear the table and clean up, anxious to put a little distance between themselves and Drew and Wes lest they change their minds.

****

"Do you have a new dress all ready for tomorrow morning, Jolie?" Drew asked after the noon meal on Saturday.

"I have a dress made, but I'm not going to church with you tomorrow," Jolie said stubbornly.

"Sure you are. I want to have the banns read, and I would like for you to attend with us."

"I don't go to church."

"Why not?"

"Because of the hypocrites like Lucy Fellows, and those two friends of hers. I know how good Church women think, and I won't be ridiculed."

"No one is going to ridicule you, Jolie," Drew said patiently.

"No they aren't. I'm not going."

"Yes, you are. I expect you to get up and get dressed in your new dress, and be ready to leave when it's time."

"I won't do it," Jolie returned, folding her arms across her chest.

Drew heard Wes yelling for him outside. "Little girl, I'll give you this afternoon to think about this. If you don't change your mind by tonight, you'll be going to church with a sore butt."

Jolie made a face at the screen door as it closed behind the aggravating man. "I'm not going to church, and he can't make me!"

"Jolie, it's not so bad to go to church. We'll just avoid Lucy Fellows. There are quite a few young women our age to socialize with, and it's fun to talk about something besides ranching. Besides, I'd like for everyone to meet my sister."

"I don't handle town and church well, Jacy. I'll end up saying or doing the wrong thing, and embarrassing you, and Drew and Wes. I would rather not go." She got up and went up to her room, leaving her sister with the clean up.

It was just a matter of time before things went terribly wrong. Jolie decided she needed to just pack up and leave. Marrying Drew was a bad idea. She'd never make the type of wife he needed. She was too used to being on her own, and doing as she pleased. She didn't wear dresses; she wore pants... and she could use a gun with the best of them. It was time to move on.

Sadly, Jolie penned a note to her sister, promising to come and visit in a few months, and then she changed into her pants, strapped on her gun, then climbed out the window and shimmied down the tree. She didn't see Drew or Wes anywhere about, so she saddled her horse, then rode out at a fast gait. She needed to find a way to earn some money, fast.

And there was only one way to do that, she decided. Drew certainly wouldn't approve, but it was her life, and she'd do as she darn well pleased. The trip into town gave her what she was after... A poster stating there was a $500.00 reward for the capture (dead or alive) of one Bernie Quail.

****

"What's wrong, Jacy?" Wes asked the minute he saw his wife's face. "You've been crying!" He hurried to take her in his arms and give her a hug. "Are you okay?"

"Where's Jolie?" Drew asked with a frown.

"She's gone," Jacy said tearfully, then took her sister's note out of her apron pocket and handed it to Drew. "She says she can't fit in here… and that's not true! I want her to stay!"

"Damn," Drew muttered under his breath. "Maybe I shouldn't have pushed her about going to church, but I thought it was time she started meeting people. Jacy, has she told you why she doesn't ever want to go to town?"

"She just says she's uncomfortable there. That our father was always drunk, and people made fun of her because of it. And that people don't want her kind around when they learn what she does for a living."

"What she does for a living?" Wes's face turned red. "Good grief, Jacy! You tellin' us that Jolie sells herself?"

"She's an innocent, little brother," Drew said without reservation. "But what the hell does she do for money?"

"I'm not sure," Jacy's lower lip trembled. "It has something to do with her gun…"

Drew looked at Wes in horror. "Can you get by a few days without me, little brother? I need to go and find that fool woman before she gets herself killed."

"You'd better cut a switch and use it every step of the way home, Drew…" Wes advised, his arm wrapped around Jacy's slender shoulders. "Damn it, marry her… Then she can't run away again!"

Drew rode out with Wes's words ringing in his ears, and decided that Jolie was coming home with his ring on her finger, even if he had to have the minister perform the ceremony while she was face down over his knee getting her bare backside paddled!

****

"Don't make any sudden moves, Quail. The poster said dead or alive, and I don't care much one way or the other which it is." Jolie slapped the cuffs on her prey, and then moved around to stand in front of him.

"Boy, you've got to listen to me. I didn't do it. I'm innocent, but if you take me back there, they'll lynch me. I swear I didn't do it."

"That isn't for me to decide, Quail," Jolie stated without emotion. "You just settle down on your blankets and get some sleep. It'll make things a lot easier on you if you cooperate."

"Kid, listen, I didn't do it. I was with someone when the bank was robbed. I wasn't within five miles of town at the time. You've got to believe me!"

Jolie listened to Bernie Quail moan and groan until she was to the point of screaming. "If you don't shut up, I'm going to gag you," she said, and meant it.

"You're awful young to be out hunting bounties, boy. And, you ain't old enough to make a decision about a man's life. If you take me back there, that banker will have them hang me without a fair trial."

In spite of herself, Jolie was caught up in the man's story. "How can you be so sure of that?"

"Because I was with his wife," he admitted with a sheepish grin. "She and I were in love years ago, and I went off to find gold and make it rich. When I didn't come back, she married him... Now that I'm back, he wants me dead. He robbed his own bank, then lied and said he saw me coming out of the bank. I was with Sally at the time, boy."

Jolie prided herself on being able to spot the truth. "Why didn't you tell the truth when you were arrested?"

"I didn't want folks to think bad of my Sally," he declared. "She's a good woman, in spite of how it looks." His eyes reflected honesty, and she found herself wavering...

"I do NOT believe what I am seeing!" Drew said from directly right behind her.

"Drew!" Jolie jumped to her feet, whirling around to face the angry man. "What are you doing here?"

"That should be fairly obvious, little girl. I came fetch my woman back home where she belongs."

"I can't go back there!" Jolie sputtered. "I'm working right now."

"What kind of work is this for a woman?" Drew demanded, advancing on her. His dark eyes were flaming, and Jolie had no trouble reading his intentions.

"It's the only thing I know how to do," she attempted to explain.

"Mister, I'm innocent. Make her let me go, please!" Bernie Quail pleaded, hoping the man would be merciful.

"You just be quiet. I'm dealing with her right now."

"Drew... Please calm down. I really need the money..."

"No, what you really need is a good spanking, and you're damned well going to get one."

"You can't!"

"You just try and stop me!" Drew took another threatening step in her direction.

Jolie reached for her gun, and leveled at the angry man. "You just stop right there! Drew! I mean it!" He grabbed the gun from her hand, and in the next instant, she was face down over his lap. Her holster was the next thing to hit the ground, and then his hand made contact with the seat of her britches. "Owwwwwwwwww! No! Stop it!"

Drew paddled her with his broad hand until his hand was hurting so badly he couldn't continue. "That, little girl, is just the beginning of the punishment you can expect for this stunt. I won't have my wife running all over the countryside chasing criminals." He pointed toward her bedroll. "Climb in there and go to sleep."

Jolie was sobbing, and had no desire to see if she could provoke another spanking. She crawled beneath the blankets, and cried herself to sleep... lying on her tummy.

"Mister, I don't blame you for walloping that girl, but what are you going to do about me...?"

Chapter Four

Drew looked at the other man and replied, "You have a poster on you, Mister. I can't very well turn you loose, now, can I?"

"But, I'm innocent, and if you take me back there, they'll lynch me without a trial… and I didn't rob that bank. Mister, if you don't help me, I'm a dead man, and I don't deserve that."

Drew snorted, and then said, "I'm not in the mood to listen to any more crap tonight. You'd better get some sleep. We're riding out of here at first light."

Jolie woke with a start, her senses telling her that something just wasn't right. She listened carefully, then whispered, "Drew, are you awake? We're getting company… You'd better pass me my gun…"

Drew was awake. He'd heard the same noises, and was pretty darn sure someone was sneaking up on the camp. He had no way of knowing how many of them there were, and he quickly picked up Jolie's gun with his left hand, while drawing his own in his right hand. "Catch," he whispered, and was relieved when Jolie caught it effortlessly, then rolled to her knees and was on her feet in the next second. Drew was ready for a fight too... In fact, Bernie Quail was the only one oblivious to the threat.

Three men came at them at once, from three different directions, guns drawn, and their target was the hapless Quail. One bullet splintered into the tree above his head, another ricocheted off a boulder. Drew took down that would be assassin with one shot, then whirled in time to see Jolie shoot down another outlaw who was trying to shoot him in the back. The third man turned to flee, and Jolie shot him in the leg.

She ran over and kicked his gun out of his hand, then pointed hers at his head. "Is there anyone else out there?" she demanded.

"Don't shoot me! Don't shoot me, please!" the man blubbered.

"Answer me!" Jolie insisted.

"No... we didn't figure it would take more than three of us to deal with Bernie and a girl!" he admitted, crying with pain.

"You figured wrong, then," Jolie was matter-of-fact. "Drew, you'd better see if you can find their horses, and make sure no one else is out there."

He didn't like being given orders by the slip of a girl, but had to admit he'd been thinking the same thing. "Jolie, when I get you home, I'm going to wear you out every day for a week. You are NEVER going to put your life at risk again. Do you hear me?"

"I'm sure every bird, fish, tree, and Comanche within a hundred miles heard you, Drew. Kindly shut up!" she dared to admonish him.

"See, I told you they were trying to kill me. These men worked for Sally's husband. He wants me dead. I tell you, I'm innocent!" Bernie pleaded with Jolie to listen to him.

"What do you have to say about this?" Jolie demanded.

"He's right, lady. Please, I've gotta have a doctor. I'm hurting real bad!"

"Who robbed the bank?" Jolie persisted in her questioning. She wasn't about to take an innocent man to a lynch mob.

"The banker did," the man squealed. "He wanted Quail framed, and dead."

"You are going to testify to that," Jolie told him, then smiled with Drew came back with three horses.

"They were alone, Jolie," he confirmed.

"We're going to go to Mason instead of Carrollton," she said without preamble. "Quail is innocent, and this man is going to testify to that. We'll let the Marshal in Carrollton deal with the banker..."

"Ain't you gonna do something about my leg?" the whiskered man whined.

****

"I've had about enough of your sass, Miss Jacy," Wes warned.

"And I've had enough of you and Drew being so damned bossy all the time. So what if Jolie doesn't want to go to church! That is her business!"

"Jacy Parker, you're beggin for a spankin'. I know you're upset about Jolie runnin' away, but you're walkin' a fine line with me."

"Everything comes down to you, doesn't it, Wesley Parker. Well, you can just do your own wash, and bake your own bread, and iron your stupid shirts! I'm going to look for my sister!" Jacy announced, then rose from the table and ran from the kitchen.

Wes fought with his temper… and lost. He just didn't tolerate that kind of behavior from his wife, and he'd be damned if she was going to go traipsing over the country side looking for that hotheaded sister of hers. He marched up the steps to their room, and was shocked to see Jacy pulling on a pair of boys' britches.

"You can take those off right now, little girl!" he thundered. "No wife of mine is going to wear pants."

"I'll wear what I please, Wes Parker. We might be married, but you do not own me!"

"I'm the head of this house, young lady, and you will obey me. Take them off, or I'll do it for you," he threatened. His answer came in the form of a heavy picture frame heaved at his head. He ducked, and it hit the wall, tearing the wallpaper in the process. "That tears it… You're gonna get a damned good spankin', little girl!"

Jacy jumped over the bed and put it between them. She could see that Wes was angry, and there was no way she was going to let him get his hands on her while he was so mad. She made a dash for the door, and then raced down the steps, Wes right after her. Out the kitchen door, and into the barn. She climbed up into the loft, and hid, trying to still her ragged breathing.

Wes knew Jacy was in the barn, and he also knew she was out of control. He was ever mindful of the pitchfork he used to clean out stalls… and he quickly looked to make sure she hadn't grabbed it to use as a weapon. She hadn't, he breathed a sigh of relief. But, she was hiding from him. He calmly took a seat on the bench beside the ladder to the loft, and settled in to wait. Miss Jacy was going to get the tanning of her life when she came down from that loft!

Jacy was trapped in the loft as long as Wes was down below sitting on that bench… unless… She crawled as quietly as possible to the back of the loft and was relieved to see the window was still open, and the rope was tied to one of the crossbeams. *Would she dare? If Jolie was in this predicament, you bet your butt she would!*

****

Wes was growing impatient. He shoved his hat back on his head and then he folded his arms across his chest. "The longer you stay up there, Jacy, the worse the reckoning." No reply. Wes waited, determined to outlast the little blonde. Fifteen minutes later he commented, "I guess you're needin' a real butt warmin', little girl. You're up to at least thirty minutes over my knee now, and I'm gonna start doubling the minutes. Each minute now is gonna add on two."

Wes was sure that would bring her down, but still no Jacy. He waited another fifteen minutes, and then slowly got to his feet. "You've just earned the spankin' of your life, Mrs. Parker," he growled, and climbed up the ladder, determined to blister her fanny. He searched everywhere, but Jacy simply wasn't in the loft. He spotted the rope hanging out the window, and then cursed. The little brat had outsmarted him!

****

Drew was happy to see the town of Mason, and shocked to his socks when the Marshal lifted Jolie off the ground and gave her a bear hug.

"Miss Jolie, you sure are a sight for these old eyes, girlie. Where you been keepin' yourself? Who's this guy?" he pointed at Drew. "Don't tell me you took on a partner?"

"Jolie is my fiancée," Drew corrected the man.

"The devil you say!" The Marshal was shocked and didn't bother to hide it. "Miss Jolie, that true?" He pointed at the bodies and the other two men. "Looks as though you had trouble... You do the shootin'?"

Drew wondered if the man was ever going to shut up so that Jolie could explain. He'd asked so many questions that he doubted the man ever listened to anyone say anything.

Jolie laughed. "It's good to see you, too, Pete. I found out I have a twin sister, and I've been staying with her and her husband, Wes. Drew, here, is Wes's older brother, and yes, we are engaged... I guess! Unless he changes his mind after seeing me in action. Don't think he likes the idea of being married to a bounty hunter. We had trouble. I went after Bernie Quail, and he said he was innocent, and this other man can testify to it. Those two were shot in self-defense when they jumped our camp and tried to kill Bernie. This man was with them and he needs a doctor. How's Miranda and the kids?"

"They're passable, Miss Jolie. You bring them on in and I'll get Doc for them two, and find the Judge. We're gonna need us some warrants..."

Over the next couple of hours Drew had to admit that Pete knew his job. And so did the Judge. He sent wires ordering the arrest of the Banker, and clearing Bernie Quail of any wrongdoing. After the legal business was all taken care of, Drew looked at the Judge and asked, "Sir, would you mind marrying Jolie and me?"

"I'd a heap rather be marrying people than hanging them!" he beamed.

Jolie was shocked, but within a few minutes she was legally Mrs. Drew Parker, and listening to her new husband telling the Judge and Pete that her bounty hunting days were coming to an end.

Pete chuckled, then warned, "Son, I've known little Miss Jolie for a long time, and she ain't gonna take much to being bossed around.

"She just promised to obey, and I intend to make sure she does just that, even if I have to spank her daily for the rest of our lives!"

****

Wes cursed as he saddled another mount. His normally sweet tempered little wife had taken HIS stallion, and, as far as he was concerned, that was the final straw. Jacy wasn't going to sit again!

****

Jacy was in trouble. Wes was going to whip her raw. She'd defied him, disobeyed him, ran from him, and taken his precious stallion. The one he'd raised from a foal and trained so patiently, the one he forbade anyone else to ride... the one the Comanche youth was stroking and planning to steal... right along with her!

Jacy knew Wes would come... and she knew that he would put his life on the line for her... and she wished she was home in her kitchen, baking his favorite cake.

****

Drew signed the hotel register, and asked that a bath be sent to their room. He could see that Jolie was nervous, and to be honest, he couldn't decide whether he was going to make love to her or give her the hiding she so richly deserved. Somehow he didn't think it would be fair to do both!

Jolie was pleased at the prospect of a bath, and she dared to hope that Drew was over his anger with her.

The tub arrived in short order, and was placed behind a privacy screen, and steaming kettles of water were poured into the tub until the cool water was nice and warm.

"You go first, Jolie," Drew told her with a smile.

She nodded, and sighed in contentment as the water enveloped her body. "This is wonderful, Drew," she called to him. "I'm pleased you thought of it."

"Do you have a nightdress in your saddle bags?" he asked, wondering what she could put on besides her dirty trail clothes.

"Yes," Jolie admitted. She'd been so anxious to sink into the tub that she'd forgotten all about what she'd put on when she got out of the tub. "Would you mind getting it for me, Drew?" she asked.

Drew was already looking for the gown. He found it, and a clean pair of britches, a shirt, socks, and under things in one side. There was also a hairbrush, and he couldn't resist slapping it against his palm. He laid out the brush where she would see it, and then draped the nightdress over the top of the privacy screen. He could hear her splashing around, and his imagination had no trouble at all picturing her... His body was quick to respond to the mental image.

Jolie hurried to finish, so that the water would still be warm for Drew. She wrapped her wet hair in a fluffy white towel, and once her body was dry, she pulled on her soft flannel gown. "I'm finished," she said as she came from behind the screen. "Your turn."

Drew nodded, and then pointed to the bed. "I laid your hairbrush right there."

"Thanks."

"You might not want to thank me in a bit. I'm still trying to decide if you're going to get that spanking you've earned tonight or when we get home."

Jolie's mouth fell open as he disappeared behind the screen. *It was her wedding night! She didn't want a spanking...!*

****

Wes circled around and once he was positive the Comanche brave was alone, he slipped in behind him, and used the butt of his gun to knock him unconscious.

"I knew you would come, Wesley," Jacy tearfully proclaimed as he cut the rawhide strips binding her hands and feet.

"Did he hurt you, honey?" Wes asked hoarsely as he held her close.

"No. Just tied me up. He was more interested in Patch."

"Let's get out of here," Wes picked her up and plopped her on Patch, then he mounted behind her. He stopped to pick up the other horse, and then moved out at a fast clip. With any luck at all the Comanche kid would head for home, and not come looking for trouble. He'd sure find it if he did!

Jacy felt safe and secure in Wes's arms, and wanted to make amends. "Wes, I'm sorry... for all of it... for getting mad at you for no reason at all, for throwing the picture at you, for disobeying you... and for running away. I'm just so worried about Jolie... but I know that doesn't excuse my behavior," she added tearfully. "Are you going to spank me?" she had to know.

"Oh yeah! You aren't going to sit for a month of Sundays," he told her. "Woman, do you know how bad you scared me?"

"I was scared, too, Wes. I knew you'd come and fight to get Patch back..."

"Patch!" Wes all but shouted. "Woman, I was worried about YOU!" Wes growled, tempted to stop the horse and flip her over and spank her butt right here and now. "Do you have any idea how scared I was that he'd already raped you? That I wasn't in time to protect you? I couldn't bear for you to be hurt, honey. You're my life, damn it!" His jaw worked emotionally, and then he scolded, "It is not safe for a woman alone out here. Why the hell do you think I forbid you to go off alone? You are NEVER going to do this again. Do you hear me?"

"Yes, sir. I promise I won't do it again, dear. I love you and I'm sorry I frightened you..."

Wes believed her. He hugged her close, and then leaned down to plant a kiss on her cheek. "I'm still going to blister your cute little butt!"

****

"I don't want a spanking on my wedding night!" Jolie pouted when Drew came around the screen, a towel hanging around his neck. All he was wearing was a pair of underwear, and she had to admit the man's chest was absolutely gorgeous.

"It might surprise you to know that I don't want to spank you, either, Jolie, but," he looked at her, "you deserve a spanking, and you're going to get one."

Jolie's eyes flashed fire, and her chin shot straight up in the air. "If you spank me, Drew Parker, I can guarantee you won't be sharing this bed with me, and there won't even be a wedding night!"

To her absolute chagrin, Drew threw back his head and laughed. "We've been married a whole hour and you're already kicking me out of bed! That has to be an all time record!"

"It's not funny, Drew," she stomped her foot in frustration.

"Jolie, I'm your husband. Your days of risking your life are over, and I mean to see you learn that lesson here and now, and every night for the next week... just like I promised you.

And, I will sleep in that bed with you tonight, and with you every night for the rest of our lives." He watched her eyes widen in fear, and he softened his voice and added, "I will never force myself on you. If we make love it will be because you want to as much as I do. You have my word on that." He paused a second to give her time to think on that, and then he held out his hand and said, "Hand me the brush, Jolie. It will do nicely..."

Jolie's eyes filled with tears, and she quickly held the brush behind her back, and out of his reach. "Please, Drew...! I don't want my wedding night spoiled with a spanking! I don't want our children to ask someday, and the only thing I have to remember is that you ruined our first night as husband and wife. It's just not the right way to start off our marriage!" she pleaded for understanding.

Jolie was a picture standing there, her long hair shining, her blue eyes bright, and that kissable pout on her lips. The last damned thing he really wanted to do was punish her, Drew realized. He was responding to her in a very physical way, and what the hell? Maybe she was right...? Maybe a spanking WASN'T the best way to start off a marriage. He stepped forward, and wrapped a single golden curl around his finger, "Do you understand that I will not tolerate your going off like this ever again, Jolie? There will be NO more bounty hunting?"

"I understand, Drew," Jolie whispered, looking into his dark eyes. His gaze was warming her with expectation. "I won't do it again, I promise."

Drew touched her cheek. "I'm going to let you off this time, Mrs. Parker, and consider it a present to both of us on our wedding night. But, if you ever, EVER, do something so reckless and foolish again, I ..." He pulled her close and kissed her passionately, his threat all but forgotten.

Jolie's relief turned into a raging need, and she returned Drew's kisses with an ardor that surprised both of them. His caresses seemed natural and there was no shame in baring herself for his pleasure. She delighted in touching him, too, and exploring his hard, masculine body. When they could no longer wait, Drew was careful of her innocence, and Jolie's pain was limited to one tiny sting, and an uncomfortable fullness that she soon became accustomed to. Drew took the time to reawaken her passion, and Jolie was first to cry out her pleasure as Drew spilled his seed within her.

****

Wes dismounted, and then lifted Jacy down to the ground. "You can come in the barn with me, Mrs. Parker."

Jacy didn't argue.

"See that bench...?" Wes pointed to the one by the loft ladder, the one he'd sat on earlier that day waiting for her to come down. "I want you to go over there, take down your britches, bare your backside, and place your palms on the bench. You will remain like that until I'm ready to whip your butt. And, Jacy, I'm warning you, this is only going to be the first of many."

Jacy didn't argue. She undid the pants and pushed them down, then untied the ribbon on her drawers and lowered them, too. She bent over and placed her hands on the bench, knowing she was fully exposed to her husband. It was embarrassing...

Wes was still shaking after he'd brushed down the horses, and cared for their needs. He glanced over toward the bench, and could see that Jacy was trembling, too, and he knew it was because she was feeling the after effects of fear, and was realizing just how close she'd come to never seeing him again. Part of him wanted to gather her up in his arms and carry her into the house and up to their bedroom and make sweet love to her, and the other part of him wanted to punish her so severely that she'd never put herself in such danger again.

Jacy could feel Wesley's eyes on her, and she wanted to turn and face him, and beg him to hold her. She was never going to ride off like that again! Never!

Wes's shaking hands went to his belt, but after a moment or two of fumbling, he realized that he simply couldn't bring himself to whip Jacy. He walked up behind her, and gave her a resounding whack on her right cheek, then pulled her upright. "Damn it, Jacy! You scared me! Don't you ever do that again, do you hear me, girl?"

Jacy nodded, upset at the tears in his eyes. She caressed his cheek, then whispered, "I give you my solemn promise, and will regard it as a vow, Wes. I won't ever do that again. I love you too much to put you through such hell."

Wes scooped her up in his arms, and headed for the house. He didn't stop until he'd lowered her on their bed, and then it was to remove his boots. "I need you, Jacy," he stated, and quickly undressed the both of them. There was no foreplay, just two people desperate to be joined together as quickly as possible. He thrust inside her with a powerful lunge, and Jacy gasped with raw need. When they were both spent, they fell into a deep sleep.

****

"Good morning, Mrs. Parker," Drew opened his eyes to see his new wife looking down at him in amusement.

"Good morning, Mr. Parker. You snore!" she grinned.

"I've been told that before," he winked. "Did I keep you awake?"

"No. It was sort of pleasant," she giggled, then snuggled close. "I like being married, so far."

"So do I," he agreed.

"I'm starving though. I was tempted to go looking for breakfast, but decided to see how long it would take you to wake up if I stared at you."

"How long did it take?" he asked curiously.

"Not long," she giggled, and then bossed, "Up and at it... I'm hungry! Do you want eggs or pancakes?" she asked seriously.

"Neither," he replied. "I want something else for breakfast..."

"What's that?" Jolie asked seriously, then giggled when he pulled her down beside him. She forgot all about being hungry when he kissed her.

****

"I must be getting soft," Wes complained when Jacy came into their bedroom, carrying a tray. "Can't believe I slept so late!"

"It isn't late, Wes. And, I thought you deserved a little pampering this morning," she smiled. She took the towel off the tray, and watched Wes smile.

"This does look good, sweet little lady." Corn meal mush fried to a crisp, and covered with maple syrup, some bacon, a cold glass of milk, and coffee, just the way he liked it. "You are spoiling me, Jacy."

"It's in order," she declared, watching him dig in. She smiled, and told herself that she was going to go through with what she decided.

"Aren't you eating?" he asked.

"I had some coffee and some toast downstairs while I was fixing your mush."

"I can't believe you don't like this, honey. It's really good," he said with enthusiasm. He enjoyed every bite, and finally noticed she was chewing on her lower lip the way she did when she had something to tell him that he wasn't going to like. He took a deep breath, then laid down his fork and looked at her. "What is it you want to tell me, Mrs. Parker?"

Her blue eyes were startled, and her cheeks turned a bright pink. "I want to say something, Wes, but I'm not sure I can..." she stammered.

"You can tell me anything, sweetheart. I love you," he was imagining all sorts of things, all of it centered around that Comanche youth who captured her yesterday. Maybe the kid hadn't raped her, but that didn't mean he didn't hurt her in some other way... "Did that brave hurt you yesterday?" he demanded, his voice sounding harsh.

"No, honey. It's nothing like that," Jacy replied, then got up off the bed and walked over to her dresser and picked up her hairbrush and brought it to him.

"I see," Wes looked at her in surprise. "I'm assuming you aren't asking me to brush your hair with this?"

"No..." Jacy couldn't bring herself to look at him. She was so embarrassed.

"Are you feeling guilty?" he asked.

"Yes, sir. I know I deserve to be punished for behaving so foolishly... and, I just wish you would do it now and have it over with..."

Wes put the tray on the table beside the bed, and then turned to look at her. Her eyes were fixed on the quilt, and her finger was nervously tracing the patterns. "You gave me your word it wouldn't ever happen again, didn't you?"

"Yes, I did, and it won't ever," Jacy said firmly.

He believed her. "I thought the fright of the experience was punishment enough. Am I wrong?"

Jacy looked up to see if he was teasing her. He wasn't. The green eyes were solemn, and she could tell he was weighing her words carefully. "I feel guilty, Wesley. You could have been killed trying to save me!" He nodded, and listened as she continued. "I was sassy, and in a temper. I was defiant... and I took Patch... just to make you mad!"

"It worked, honey," he nodded. "I was plenty mad. If I'd caught up to you right away, you would have had the tanning of your life."

"I know..."

The blue eyes were full of guilt, and Wes promptly decided that Jacy needed a good spanking so that she could forgive herself. "Very well, young lady. Just know that I intend to do a thorough job of this. You can pull up that gown and put yourself right over my knee.

Jacy did as she was told, reminding herself that she'd asked for this spanking. Wes quickly started spanking her, using the hairbrush over and over and over again until her backside and thighs were sore and throbbing.

"That should take care of the sassing and the tantrum," he said quietly. "Now we'll deal with the fact you ran from me. Go and get my belt and bring it here."

Jacy couldn't believe he was going to strap her, too, but there was no mistaking the determination in his tone of voice. Wes didn't do things by half-measures. He was going to make this a punishment she would remember, even if she did ask him for it. She picked up his belt and brought it to him.

Wes doubled the belt, and then patted his left thigh. "I want that red butt of yours right here, little lady. You're going to get a good licking now, the one you would have had in the barn yesterday if you'd climbed down from that loft..."

Jacy crawled over Wes's lap, and wasn't surprised when he pushed her forward and used his right leg to trap her legs between his. He grabbed her right wrist, and pulled her body tight against his so that she couldn't squirm. She very much feared she was in for a long, hard strapping. "How many?" she asked fearfully.

"Yesterday I intended to spank you with my hand for as long as you spent in the loft, and then give you one lick of my belt for each minute you were up there. Since you had the hairbrush instead of my hand, I cut that spanking in fourth. But, I sat below that loft for at least an hour. I reckon that means you get sixty with my belt."

The most he'd ever given her was forty, and Jacy was unbelievably sore then... She'd already had the hairbrush, and there was simply no way she could handle sixty with his belt. The first one took her breath away, and try as she might, she couldn't twist away. All she could do was cry out each time the belt landed a fiery red strip across her butt and thighs. She was soon sobbing, and begging Wes to stop, but he didn't listen. He gave her sixty, then stood her on her feet and sent her to the corner to think about what was next.

Jacy was miserable. Her poor fanny was on fire, and Wes seemed determined to punish her thoroughly. She couldn't really blame him. She'd been very foolish, but she was sorry, and she'd had more than enough. She couldn't imagine what he would do next, but surely getting captured by the Comanche brave was worse than hiding in the loft? How was she going to get through this? Why did she ever open her mouth...?

Wes looked at Jacy's poor butt and felt sorry for her. He hated punishing her like this, but they both knew it was deserved. He was afraid that if he didn't take the time to impart a good lesson, the next time Jacy felt like defying him, she would go right ahead and do it! He was going to have to be very firm, whether he liked it or not.

****

Drew and Jolie were seated at a table, having their breakfast, when they heard shots outside. Drew made a grab for Jolie, but she reached the door, gun in hand, before he had time to do more than call, "Jolie!" He gave chase, his intention to protect her from whatever was happening out in the street.

He was just in time to see several men firing shots in their general direction, and Jolie returning fire. "They robbed the bank and shot Sheriff Pete!" she filled him in, and then rose up to shoot again as four men hightailed it out of town. "You take care of Pete. I'm going after them!"

Drew grabbed for the feisty blonde again, and missed! She was already mounted on Pete's horse, giving chase. Drew cursed, checked to make sure someone was caring for the disabled lawman, and then sprinted toward the livery to get his horse. He was going to tear a strip off Jolie's backside when he caught up to her... if the outlaws didn't shoot her first!

****

The outlaws were riding hard and fast, and Jolie decided that she'd be better off to slow down a bit so that she didn't ride into a trap. There were four of them, and it was hard telling how long it would take Pete's deputy to get a posse together to come with some help. She continued to trail them, and could spot their dust up ahead several times.

Jolie forced her mind to stay on the job, and not on her husband's probable reaction to the fact she'd ridden out of town, chasing an outlaw gang. She'd never convince him that this was the sort of thing she did best, and that it was as natural as breathing to her. She spotted dust up ahead, and decided to risk moving in a bit closer. They would probably split up soon... and she needed to be close enough to see who took the money.

****

Drew was going to cut ten switches and use them all! He was going to use his belt then, and when his arm was tired, he was going to turn her around, and use his left hand on her butt until he couldn't raise his arm at all! How dare she do something so foolish? And right after she promised him she wouldn't!?!! He was going to stand her in a corner for a month of Sundays, and then he would whip her butt again!

He finally caught sight of her up ahead, and felt his temper rise to the challenge. A good tanning is exactly what the little brat needed and was going to get! As he was contemplating the satisfaction he would get from turning her bare butt up over his knee, he saw a man step out from behind a rock and take aim at Jolie's back! Drew let out a whoop of warning, but the man fired, and Jolie fell off her horse.

****

"What do you have to say for yourself, young lady?" Wes asked, directly behind his wife.

"I'm sorry, Wes... Honestly and truly." She was sorry.

"I believe you, honey," he turned her around so that he could look at her. "Your butt isn't going to like sitting down anytime soon, is it?"

"No, sir," she tearfully agreed.

"By rights, I should give you another tanning for lighting out of here on Patch," he told her, taking his handkerchief and wiping her face. "Do you agree with me?" he wanted to know.

"Yes, sir." He was right, and she didn't have the right to ask him to be merciful.

"The truth is, honey, I can't do that. You've had enough of a spanking to last you for a few days, and if I was to tan you again right now, I'd feel like I was being mean to you." He leaned down and kissed the top of her head. "I'm going to give you another punishment, and I'm afraid you aren't gonna like it… but it stands," he said firmly. "For the next month, you'll fix supper early, eat yours, and then go straight to bed."

"Noooooooooooooo!" Jacy protested. "Oh, Wes… You know how I hate to go to bed early! Please don't make me do that!!! Please! I'd rather have another strapping…. Please???" She'd never survive a whole month of being sent to bed early. The few times Wes had punished her that way, she'd hated it!!!

"Jacy, I warned you that you wouldn't like it. You aren't supposed to, that's the whole purpose of callin' it a punishment."

"Oh, Wesley, please… anything else but that… Or make it for one night only… not for a whole month! That is meaner than spanking me would be!" she declared. "You know that evenings are our only time together, and that I teach Jolie to write… I won't be able to do anything if I'm in bed!"

"Except think. And that is what I want you to do." He put his fingers over her mouth when she started to say something else. "I don't want to hear another word, young lady. You've been spanked enough for one day, but don't think I can't find a stall or two for you to muck out if you keep sassing me. You will be in bed by six o'clock for the next month, with no further argument. Defy me, or disobey me, and you will regret it."

Jacy burst into tears, and Wes let her cry. This was one time he was going to be firm.

Chapter Five

Drew rode in closer, his heart beating furiously, took aim, and felled the outlaw. He jumped from his mount and ran to where Jolie lie on the ground. "Jolie! Jolie!"

To his shock, she rolled over, and looked at him. "Did you get him, Drew?" she demanded.

"Yes. Where are you hurt?" he demanded, looking for blood.

"He missed. I jumped off when I heard your shout, or he would have had me!" she admitted. "Thanks!"

"You're okay?" Drew asked in disbelief, raising her up to check her back.

"Other than feeling stupid for letting him circle back and take a shot at me. We need to get after the other three. They must be getting close to their hideout, or they wouldn't have tried to stop me."

"You aren't going anywhere!" Drew said forcefully.

"I have to track them, Drew. I owe it to Pete!" she argued.

"You will let the law deal with this, Mrs. Parker."

"Sure, just as soon as the posse catches up," she agreed, sensing some placating was in order. Drew's dark eyes were fairly snapping with temper, and she feared she was in serious trouble.

"NOW!" he raised his voice.

"Drew, be reasonable. What harm will it do to track those men to their hideout? They think I'm dead now... and they'll be waiting on that one to catch up. By the time they realize he isn't coming, we'll have them. Come on... I could use some help here."

"You could use a good tanning," he argued.

"That won't help catch the bank robbers," she pointed out, smiling for his benefit.

Drew didn't know how she did it, but he found himself riding along beside her, trailing the gang who robbed the bank. "I swear, little girl, when this is over, you're going to get your butt blistered good and proper."

****

Wes wiped his brow, unable to shake the uneasy feeling that had been plaguing him all morning. He'd gone up to the house a couple times to check on Jacy. She was pouting, mad as hell at him for giving her an early bedtime, but she didn't seem sick... or like she was planning to take off on him. Her replies to his questions had been brief, but she hadn't given him any reason to threaten her with another consequence.

He pounded another nail into the fence he was repairing, and then noticed a buggy approaching the ranch. He paused to see who it was, and finally made out Pastor Fellows' solid form. Wes cursed under his breath, and headed for the house. This was not a good time for the minister to bring his wife to call.

"We have company, Jolie," he stated without preamble. "I expect you to behave yourself, or else. Is that understood?"

"I'm not a child, Wesley Parker! Even though you seem to think I am!"

"Misbehave now, and I'll make it two months." He hoped the warning would suffice, and went outside to greet their guests.

"Hello, Wes. I hope we haven't called at a bad time?" Jacob Fellows asked in his deep voice.

"Not at all. Would you like to come inside and have something cool to drink?" he offered politely.

"That would be nice, wouldn't it, Lucy?" the man looked at his sullen wife.

"If we must," she sniffed.

Jacy's blue eyes went to Wes the moment she spotted their guests, but she promptly plastered a smile on her face, and greeted them politely, asking them to take a seat.

Lucy Fellows went to the sofa and made a big to-do about sitting there, perching on the edge of the seat as if she was afraid she would soil her dress.

Wes bit his tongue, determined to set a good example for his wife. "It's sure been hot, hasn't it?" he asked.

"Yes, indeed," Jacob replied, and then came to the point. "We missed you and your family at church Sunday, and I thought perhaps Lucy and I needed to come and discuss the situation, and see if we can't resolve the differences between the ladies. Lucy would be pleased to speak to Mrs. Parker and her sister..." The last was said with a stern look in his wife's direction.

Jacy entered carrying a tray with glasses of lemonade and a plate of freshly baked cookies. "My sister isn't home at the moment."

"Good!" Lucy muttered into her handkerchief, speaking a bit louder than she intended, and earning another look from her husband. "I mean, that is too bad, but good that you are here..."

"What is it you wish to say to my wife, Mrs. Fellows?" Wes asked directly as Jacy passed the plate of cookies around.

"Jacob thinks it best that I apologize for the misunderstanding between us." She took a cookie from the plate, took a bite, and coughed and sputtered. "Oh, dear! I should give you my recipe!" she smiled malevolently.

Wes felt his temper flare, especially when he saw the hurt in his wife's lovely blue eyes. "There is nothing wrong with Jacy's cookies, Mrs. Fellows. If you came to apologize, get to it. I won't have you sniping at Jacy."

"Well, I never!" the woman gasped.

"Lucy Fellows, I warned you!" Jacob bellowed. "I brought you here to apologize to this child, and you are going to do so, even if I have to take a strap to you here and now!"

"Jacob, how dare you speak to me like this in front of them?" Lucy dabbed her handkerchief at her eyes to stem nonexistent tears. "I've already apologized, and was treated abominably by this young man! How can you subject me to this humiliation? I told you what she and that evil sister of hers did!"

"Pastor, I'm sorry your wife is such a shrew, but I won't have her in my home unless she can treat Jacy and Jolie with respect." Wes got to his feet.

"Young man, I agree with you wholeheartedly. I was so busy tending my parish that I forgot to tend to my wife, and she's grown completely out of control. If you will excuse us but a moment, I would like to borrow your barn. Perhaps in a few minutes, Lucy will be able to return and offer an apology that is sincere and heartfelt."

Wes nodded in understanding. "Help yourself, sir. There's a nice leather strap hanging by the bench under the loft. Feel free to borrow it."

Lucy's face was a mottled red when Jacob grabbed her arm and hauled her to her feet. "No, Jacob! It isn't necessary. I will apologize."

"Yes, you will apologize..." Jacob marched her out of the house and to the barn.

"I can't believe that Pastor Fellows is going to whip his wife here and now!" Jacy shivered with sympathy. Her own bottom was still aching unbearably, and she wasn't able to sit without flinching. She couldn't wish a sore fanny on anyone right now!

"She deserves a good tanning," Wes was without sympathy. He picked up a cookie, and tasted it. "These are good, honey. That old biddy was just being mean to you."

"Which is why I called her a 'mean old witch' in the first place," Jacy commented. "She is mean."

"But you are a lady, and I will be pleased to have you remember that when she is around," Wes warned, then pulled her into his arms to give her a hug. He kissed her lightly, and was pleased when she started to respond.

Jacy returned his kiss, then whispered, "Honey, please... Don't make me go to bed early... Please... I swear I will never ever risk my life like that again. I promise."

Wes looked down into her pleading blue eyes, and then deliberately swatted her sore fanny, causing her to squeal. "I don't want to hear another word on the subject, young lady. You are being punished, and that is final." The tears filling her eyes made him feel guilty, but Wes was positive he was doing the right thing.

****

Jacob Fellows pulled the struggling Lucy into the barn, and over to the bench beside the ladder to the loft. Just as Wes promised, there was a leather strap hanging there. "You can raise your skirts, wife."

"Please don't do this, Jacob!" Lucy begged.

"Raise your skits, Lucy, or I will do it for you."

"I'm a grandmother! Why is it so wrong to expect those young women to be respectful?" she whimpered.

"It's wrong because you're being hateful, Lucy. You never used to be like that, and I won't have it now. That child offered you a cookie, and you practically spit it out! Even if it was terrible, you should have been gracious, but, Lucy, that cookie was as good as yours and you know it! I'm disappointed in you, and I'm going to repeat this lesson as often as necessary until my sweet wife returns." He brought the strap down hard over her skirt, and Lucy jumped. "Raise your skirts, and lower your drawers, wife. If I have to do it, I will, and you will receive an extra dose of strap."

Lucy slowly raised her skirts. "Please, Jacob, let me keep my drawers... Someone could walk in."

"I fully intended to do just that, until you fussed at me. Now you will lower them."

Lucy did as he said, crying with mortification. Jacob raised one foot to the bench and bent Lucy over his thigh and held her there with his left arm around her waist. "I regret this is necessary, wife, but you need to mind your sharp tongue."

Lucy hollered as Jacob whipped her, begging him repeatedly to stop. He continued to lay the strap over her ample bottom and thighs until there wasn't a spot of white left, and he still continued to apply the strap.

"Am I making an impression, my dear?" he demanded.

"Yes, sir! I'm so sorry!" Lucy sobbed.

"I'm sure you are. And you will be even sorrier..."

"Oh, Jacob, please! I can't bear this!"

"You have shamed me with your behavior..."

"I will apologize!" she proclaimed.

"Yes, you will," he calmly agreed. SPLAT!!

"Please forgive me, Jacob!" Lucy's cries were desperate now.

"Do you think you can remember to conduct yourself in a manner befitting my wife?" he asked with a particularly hard crack on her sit spot.

"Owwwwwwww! Oh, yes, sir! I will be very good from now on."

"Very well. To prove you've learned your lesson, you will ask for another dozen to remind you of your promise. And you will count them and thank me for them."

Lucy cried harder, but knew she wouldn't be leaving the barn until she did as Jacob said. "Please give me another twelve to remind me of my promise, Jacob."

"Very well, my dear. Count loudly so that I can hear you."

The first one landed on her thighs and Lucy wailed. "One. Thank you, sir."

Jacob was patient, and gave Lucy plenty of time to count each stroke, but eventually she was crying too hard to count, and he said, "You've done well, Lucy. I'll give you the last four now, and we'll be all done."

Lucy was positive this was an experience she did not want to repeat. The last four landed on the same spot, and the pain was unbearable. Jacob helped her to stand, and held her while she cried.

"You may fix your clothing, my dear… Then we will go inside and make your apologies."

****

Jolie sighed as she glanced at Drew. He was sitting rigid in his saddle, and she knew he was angry with her. She would simply have to deal with him later, she decided. The outlaws were right ahead, and she was positive they'd separate soon. She would need to be there when they did that.

Drew was trying to keep his mind on what they were about. He didn't like permitting his bride to ride into a dangerous situation, but if the town was to recover their money, it seemed it would be up to them to help. Surely that Deputy Sheriff would be along soon with a posse, and he could take Jolie back to the hotel and spend the rest of the day teaching her a well deserved lesson.

"We need to stop, Drew," she suddenly reached out and touched his arm, speaking in a whisper. "They're going to split up and go their separate ways."

Before he realized what she intended to do, Jolie tied her mount to a bush, and then took off on foot. "Damn it, Jolie Parker! You come back here!"

"Would you be quiet before you get us killed, Drew!" Jolie whispered. "I need your help, and your fussing at me is making it hard to concentrate!"

"Jolie, sweetie, you are going to wish you'd never been born when I get you back to town," he growled.

"Oh, for Pete's sake!" she threw up her hands in exasperation. "Go back to the horses and wait there!" She turned on her heel and headed toward the outlaws.

Drew fought to control his temper. He wanted to grab her and shake her senseless, but knew he didn't dare. He followed behind her, and nearly stumbled over her when she stopped abruptly.

"How much do you think we got?" one of the outlaws asked excitedly.

"Must be several thousand here," another declared.

"Max should have been back by now," the third man looked around him uneasily.

"Aww, you know Max. That was a female following us, and he's probably having himself some fun with her."

Jolie felt her cheeks turn pink, and she felt Drew stiffen in rage at the very thought of the outlaw touching her. She took a deep breath, and pulled her gun, stepping into the clearing. "You're under arrest. Drop your guns!"

One of the men went for his gun, and she shot it out of his hand. Drew joined her by then, and the other two men put their hands into the air.

Drew took their guns and tied their hands behind their backs. He didn't dare look at Jolie right now. When they reached town, she was in for the lesson of her short life.

They ran into the posse about a half hour later, and the deputy gladly took charge of the prisoners, pleased as could be that the money had been recovered. "We sure are obliged to ya, Miss Jolie," he said. "Ole Pete will be proud."

Jolie shrugged dismissively, "I was just in the right place, Tom."

Drew stayed right beside her on the ride back to town, and once the horses were stabled, he took her hand in his and led her back to the hotel. He stopped at the desk, and said, "If you hear screaming, ignore it. My wife is going to get her butt whipped raw!"

****

"I am very sorry I was so rude to you, Mrs. Parker," Lucy Fellows said the minute they were back inside the parlor. "I hope you and your sister will feel welcome to come back to church this Sunday."

"Is that all, my dear?" Jacob frowned.

"No... I was mean about your cookies. They really are very good," Lucy admitted, and then looked at Jacob. "Is that everything, Jacob?" He just raised an eyebrow, and Lucy thought for a second, and added, "I also apologize for pretending I couldn't walk. It wasn't very nice... and Jacob has reminded me that I need to be more considerate of everyone's feelings. I am truly sorry I've been so hateful towards you, and I hope you'll give me another chance to prove that I have some manners."

Jacy couldn't help but feel sorry for the older woman. They'd been out in the barn for a very long time, and the woman's eyes were red-rimmed from crying. Since she didn't have much use for sitting at the moment herself, Jacy was inclined to be forgiving. "It wasn't nice of me to call you a 'mean old witch', either, Mrs. Fellows, and I regret doing so. Perhaps we should just start all over...?" she smiled.

Lucy knew she was being offered an olive branch and she gratefully accepted it. "Thank you, Jacy. I would like that."

"So would I..." Jacy smiled again. "Would you like to stay and share a meal with us?"

"No!" Lucy replied hastily, before her husband could accept. "I'm not feeling... well... at the moment..."

"Lucy is reluctant to sit at the table, I'm afraid," Jacob explained. "I'm sure the buggy ride home is going to be difficult enough for her. We'll bid you good day, and hope you'll join us Sunday."

"We'll be there, Pastor Fellows," Wes replied. He and Jacy walked the other couple to their buggy, and Wes tried to hide his grin when the woman sat down and let out a gasp as her inflamed backside met the leather seat.

"Would you like to borrow a pillow, ma'am?" Jacy offered graciously.

"Please...?" Lucy looked toward her husband.

"Now, my dear, you should know that I won't permit that," the man said kindly, then turned to Wes and added, "It does no good to take the time to punish them if they have a nice soft pillow to sit upon."

"I agree, sir," Wes's expression said that Jacy should have known better than to make the offer.

"Well, there's no harm in being tenderhearted," Jacob said with a warm smile for Jacy. "You are a sweet young lady to offer..." He clicked to the horse, and off they went.

"I couldn't help but feel sorry for her, Wesley. They have a long trip back into town, and I have a feeling he really laid into her."

"She deserved a good hiding," Wes wasn't inclined to waste any sympathy on the woman. He pulled out his watch and looked at it. "You have exactly two hours to have supper fixed, yours eaten, and get yourself in bed."

"Wes, I can't do that! I have so much to do yet today! I'm sewing a dress for Jolie, and I have a letter to write... I can't get everything done in two hours, and it won't be dark until at least nine!!! Please let me stay up until it gets dark. That is still way too early to go to bed, but I'll do it and not argue about it..." she suggested. "Please, honey! Six o'clock is just too early!" When he didn't immediately agree, she continued. "Please, honey! Six o'clock is just too early!" Jacy repeated her request, and suddenly realized she'd crossed a line with her husband. He was frowning, and that did not bode well for her. "I'm sorry... I shouldn't have asked..."

"That's right. I've warned you several times that I wouldn't be talked out of punishing you with an early bedtime, young lady, and yet you've persisted in arguing with me. You can march yourself in the house and take yourself off to bed right now."

"Now?" she repeated. "But what about supper?"

"You aren't getting any," he said firmly. "Now go!"

The idea of going to bed at four o'clock in the afternoon was unthinkable, and Jacy was angry with Wes. He'd change his mind in a bit when he couldn't find anything for his supper. She stomped upstairs, and flopped down in the rocking chair beside the window, only to jump up when her poor butt met the seat. "Owwwww!" she rubbed her posterior. Surely, Wes didn't expect her to go to bed right now...? She wasn't the least bit sleepy or tired. She found some shirts that needed mending, and carefully eased her bottom down in the rocker once more. She would attach the buttons, and when Wes came to her in a bit, wanting something to eat, she would smile and be gracious, and fix him a good supper.

Wes finished mending the corral fence and decided it would behoove him to go inside and check on his wife. He didn't think she would dare to defy him, but given her sassy attitude lately, he wasn't taking her obedience for granted. Jacy despised going to bed at night, and would stay up late every night if he permitted her to do so. This next month was going to be a test of his patience, he feared, but he wanted to make the lesson one she wouldn't forget for the rest of her life. He suspected he would end up having to spank her a few times to enforce it, but little Jacy was going to learn that he took her safety seriously.

He opened the door to their room quietly, and was surprised to see her sitting in the rocker, doing some mending. She hadn't even unpinned her hair, or changed into her gown, and the bed was still made up. He shut the door behind him, and was shocked when she looked over at him and smiled.

"Are you hungry, dear? I'll be down to fix you something in a moment..." she gave him another smile.

"Jacy, where are you supposed to be?" he asked pointedly, his hands on his hips.

"Wes! It's just four-thirty! I'm not tired or sleepy. I can't go to bed!" She looked up at him, and then said, "Please, honey... Let me fix supper for us... I will be so good. I learned my lesson, I promise you I did!"

Wes shook his head. "Jacy Parker, I've had it. You are going to bed, and you're going to regret not doing it when I told you to." He crossed the room and pulled her from the chair, and over to the bed.

Jacy tried to pull free, but Wes was too strong. He sat on the bed, flipped up her skirts, and in seconds, he'd lowered her drawers down to her ankles. "Oh no, Wes!!! I'm really sore!" she protested, but Wes's hard hand landed on her right cheek with a loud crack. "Owwwww!" He continued to spank her cheeks until she was sobbing, and then he started on her thighs. "I'm sorry! I'm sorry!" she tried to wiggle off his lap, but he wasn't having it.

"You will do as you are told, and that means getting ready for bed and going when I tell you to." He concentrated on her sit spot next, and only when she collapsed over his knee in utter exhaustion did he stop. "You have five minutes to be in this bed, young lady." He rolled her off his knee, and then stomped out of the bedroom.

Jacy wasn't about to push Wes any farther. She removed her clothing and slipped into her gown, then unpinned her hair and brushed it out. She loosely braided it, then turned down the quilt and climbed into bed. She settled on her tummy, and was barely under the sheet when the door opened again. The look on Wes's face was formidable, and she shuddered to think what he would have done if she hadn't obeyed him this time.

Wes walked over to her, leaned down until he was in her face, and said firmly, "You will be in bed by six pm for the next month, Jacy. Arguing with me, sassing at me, fussing with me, or defying me will earn you an earlier bedtime and a freshly spanked backside. You can accept this punishment as due, or you can make it much harder on yourself. The choice is yours.

Do not leave this bed for any reason until I give you permission in the mornings. Do you understand me?" he demanded.

"Yes, sir," she said meekly.

Wes leaned down and kissed her, then turned on his heel and left the room, closing the door on her sobs. He wasn't going to survive the next month!

****

"I don't suppose you'd be willing to put off this discussion until after we have some supper, Drew?" Jolie asked consideringly. "Neither of us finished breakfast, and it's time for supper now... I know you're as hungry as I am...?"

Drew didn't answer her. His hands went to his belt buckle, and he watched Jolie back up a few steps as she read his intention in his eyes.

Jolie ran her tongue over her lips, and then said, "I don't suppose I can talk you into waiting until we get home...? It is our honeymoon..."

"I let you off against my better judgment last night. I'm not going to make that mistake today."

"It was our wedding night, and you did the right thing. I didn't break my promise to you, either, Drew. I didn't go after bounty..." she pointed out.

"No, you formed a posse of one and went after bank robbers who just shot the Sheriff!" Drew roared.

"I knew you'd come along to help," she smiled in an effort to placate him, but when he slid the belt from the loops on his pants, she knew it hadn't made the slightest bit of difference to him.

"You can get those britches off right now, little girl..."

Jolie looked up at him, and felt the tears forming in her eyes. She tried to blink them away, then whispered, "This marriage isn't going to work, Drew. I'm not a lady... I react to situations like the one today. It's just the way I am, and I can't help it. I don't think it's fair that you whip me for that."

Drew looked at her, and then shook his head, "It's not going to work. You are a married woman, Jolie, and you're going to act like one. I don't give one royal damn what that idiot father of yours let you get away with, you are not going to pull stunts like the one you did today and get away with it. I love you, and you're going to find out just how much!" he tapped the belt against his leg. "Get those pants off."

Jolie looked at him, marveling at his words. She pulled off her boots, and then stood to remove her pants. "You're telling me that you're going to punish me because you love me?"

"That's right. I love you enough to expect you to obey me, Jolie, and not risk your life every time you turn around."

Jolie looked at him again, then said, "I've never had anyone care before, Drew..." She untied the ribbon on her drawers, and then asked, "Do you think you could love me with your hand instead of your belt? I'm really new to this marriage business... and I think I would feel just as loved if you took it easy..."

Drew couldn't help it. He laughed. The little minx was playing him for all she was worth, and damned if she wasn't doing a good job of it! He walked over to sit on the bed, and patted his thigh. "Right here, young lady." To his surprise, Jolie laid herself over his lap.

"Drew, I didn't mean to scare you today. I'm sorry for that," she acknowledged, then yelped when he started spanking her in earnest. The smacks were hard, and it was obvious the man meant business. She was going to have one toasty butt by the time he finished.

"You are never to chase after outlaws again..." Drew scolded, spanking her with slaps meant to sting like fire. His hand was burning already, and he'd barely begun! He decided that he wasn't going to impart the lesson she deserved by using just his hand, so he put her on her feet and escorted her to an empty corner. "You stand right here, Mrs. Parker, and think about what could have happened to you today."

Jolie didn't argue. As long as she was standing in the corner, he was leaving her poor bottom alone. She was sure she had his handprints all over her fanny, and hoped that standing in the corner would be the end of the punishment... but knowing Drew, she doubted it. He was a master at coming up with additional punishments designed to make her think. All of a sudden she remembered that her hairbrush was lying on the dresser, and she had a pretty good idea that she was going to have a session with it before this was all over...

"Well, Jolie? What could have happened to you today?" Drew asked from directly behind her.

"Drew, I was thinking about you and that's why that outlaw was able to slip behind me without my knowing," she explained. "I was hoping you wouldn't be too upset with me..."

"If I hadn't yelled, he would have killed you!" Drew said emotionally. "Do you have any idea how scared I was when I saw you fall to the ground?"

"I'm sorry," she whispered, feeling very small.

"Not as sorry as you will be in a few minutes," he predicted. "I'm going to give you a choice, Jolie. You can walk over to that bed, pile the pillows and put your butt up there for a good strapping with my belt. Or you can choose the hairbrush, and I will hold you over my knee. Neither is going to be a picnic. If you choose the belt, it will be over much sooner, than if you choose the hairbrush."

Jolie turned around to face him, and reached up to caress his cheek. "It's my choice to let you decide whatever you think is fair," she whispered, accepting it as his right to do so.

"If I decide, little one, you'll get a healthy dose of hairbrush, and then a few good licks of my belt."

He watched her blue eyes widen, but she squared her slender shoulders. "I'll accept whatever you decide, Drew."

He led her over to the bed, and turned her over his knee. The hairbrush left a brightly colored oval wherever he smacked it against her bottom and her thighs, and he continued spanking her hard until his arm was tired.

Jolie was sobbing from the pain of the spanking, and wondered how she would make it through a strapping, too, but she would. She owed it to him to repay him for scaring him so badly. If their marriage was going to work, she had to make an effort to adapt to Drew's rules... and punishments.

Drew placed the pillows on the bed, and then told Jolie to get into position. He was pleased that she did so without a single protest, and decided that perhaps he could lighten up a little. "I was going to give you twenty-five, but since you're accepting this so well, honey, I'm only going to give you ten. They will be fast and hard, and right where you sit. I expect you to stay in place and accept them."

Jolie nodded in understanding, and Drew was true to his word. Each slap of the belt on her tender skin blazed like fire, and staying in place was the hardest thing she'd ever done. It was over soon, and when it was, Drew dropped his belt and pulled her into his arms. He held her while she cried, and Jolie decided he was right. She did feel loved and cherished, and knew she would always feel this way when he held her.

Chapter Six

  Wes slipped upstairs several more times throughout the long evening, and found Jacy just as he left her. She'd been crying for hours, and he was feeling about as guilty as he could. He knew how much he'd hated being sent to bed when he was a kid, and had to imagine it was even worse as a grown woman. And, damned if she hadn't pushed him into spanking her after he said he wouldn't. He'd done without supper, and finally decided to go to bed early himself. He couldn't concentrate on the bookwork, and he didn't feel like reading. He missed having Jacy sitting across the room from him.

  Jacy heard Wes coming upstairs again, and knew he was checking up on her. She felt terrible for giving him such a hard time earlier, but doubted he would believe her if she told him. She lay perfectly still when he came into the room. She'd heard the clock strike nine a few minutes ago, and she'd been lying here, wide awake, for nearly five hours now. She needed to relieve herself, but wasn't sure that Wes would permit her that small comfort after her earlier defiance.

"Jacy, if you need to tend to business, you can get up to take care of it," Wes offered, then smiled to himself when she tossed back the sheet and hurried to the other side of the screen to use the chamber pot they kept in the room for nighttime. "Feel better?" he asked when she returned to bed.

"Yes, thank you," she answered, and was surprised when she heard his boots hit the floor. "Are you coming to bed?" she asked.

"No law says I can't," he smiled at her. "I missed my wife..."

"Wes, I'm sorry about earlier," Jacy said tearfully. "I just hate going to bed early, and I shouldn't have given you a hard time over it. I promise I won't do it again. Will you forgive me?" she wanted to know.

"I already have," he replied, then pulled her close to hug her. He was pleased when she kissed him, and he kissed her back. "Are you sure you aren't too sore for this, sweetheart?" he asked hoarsely, aching with need as she pressed her warm body against his.

"I was afraid you'd tell me 'no' for the next month," she admitted, then threw herself into pleasing her husband.

****

Jolie sat gingerly in her saddle. The trip was going to be long and arduous, but she was determined to make it without complaint. Drew informed her that he needed to get back to the ranch because Wes needed his help, and that meant she would have to sit her saddle, comfortable or not. She knew he considered it an extension of her punishment, and deserved.

He did permit her to go by and check on Pete, and she was relieved to see him sitting up in bed, enjoying the pampering his wife and daughters were lavishing on him. He told her to be good, and listen to her new husband, and Jolie was pretty darn sure that everyone in town knew her husband had spanked her soundly.

After a few days on the trail, they finally arrived at the ranch, and Jacy ran outside to give her a big hug. "Don't you ever run away from us again!" she scolded.

"I hope you tanned her good and proper, brother?" Wes asked darkly, remembering how his own sweet woman had tried to go after Jolie and been captured by the Comanche brave.

"I wedded her, bedded her, and beat her butt soundly," Drew announced, then chuckled when his brother's mouth dropped open in shock.

"Oh, Jolie!! Is that true? Are you and Drew really married?" Jacy asked with a giggle. "Oh, you are! I can see it in your eyes!" She hugged and kissed Jolie, then kissed Drew. "Isn't this wonderful, Wes?" she asked excitedly.

"It'll do," Wes drawled, and then grinned at his brother. He shook his hand, and then gave Jolie a peck on the cheek. "You treat my brother right, now, or you'll be answering to me!"

"I will, Wes," Jolie promised, her eyes sparkling.

"Supper is almost ready," Jacy announced, and then looked over at Wes with a stricken expression. "Please, honey? Just this once, since it's a special occasion?"

"No, ma'am. It stands, and no exceptions. You have about twenty minutes, so you'd best hurry up and eat your supper."

Jacy's eyes filled with tears, but she didn't argue with her husband. She hurried inside, and hurriedly dished up a plate of stew and sat at the table to eat it.

"What's going on, Jacy?" Jolie followed her inside and watched as Jacy tearfully served her meal.

"I'm being punished, Jolie. I have to be in bed in exactly seventeen minutes, and if I'm not, Wes will spank me and put me to bed..."

"Why?" Jolie asked, and listened in disbelief as Jacy explained. "That isn't fair!" she declared, and was out the door and on her way to the barn before Jacy could stop her.

Drew and Wes looked up as Jolie came stomping into the barn, her hands on her hips, and her blue eyes blazing. She marched right up to Wes and hauled off and kicked him as hard as she could on the shin.

"Owwwwwwwww!" Wes hollered as he grabbed his leg and hopped on one foot.

"Jolie Parker! What is this all about?" Drew grabbed her arm and pulled her around to face him.

"Your brother is a tyrant!" Jolie accused. "And I'm going to fix him good!" She tried to pull free of Drew, but he held her tight. "You let me go!"

"Don't you kick me, little girl!" Drew warned, reading the intent in her eyes. "You just settle right now and tell me what this is all about!" he ordered sharply, trying to tune out Wes's curses.

"He's making Jacy go to bed at six o'clock every evening for a month!" Jolie accused.

Drew looked over at Wes, shocked. "Good grief, man... Six o'clock? What the heck did she do to deserve that?"

"She ran off to go and find her sister," Wes explained, "and she was taken captive by a Comanche brave..." His green eyes were full of temper. "This is between Jacy and me, Drew. The punishment stands." He headed for the door, and then turned, "I suggest you tell Miss Jolie here that I don't cotton to being kicked. Next time I just might forget myself and tan her backside for her."

"Drew! It's not fair! He's being mean to Jacy!" Jolie insisted. "You need to do something."

"Jolie, Jacy isn't like you. She can't take care of herself at all. She's damn lucky Wes found her in time. Wes doesn't have a mean bone in his body where Jacy is concerned, and you need to butt out."

"I can't do that, Drew!"

"Yes, you can and you will..."

"Jacy hates going to bed!" Jolie's eyes filled with tears. "You don't understand, Drew... This isn't a punishment, it's cruel... I can't stand it... It's all my fault. I'd rather have Wes punish me than Jacy..." She started crying, and Drew pulled her close and held her.

****

Jacy wasn't the least bit surprised when Wes entered the bedroom to check on her. He did so each and every night. But this time his face was set in angry lines, and she feared she was in for a spanking for asking him to let her off tonight. "I'm sorry I asked to be let off tonight, Wes. I didn't mean to anger you."

"I'm not angry at you, sweetie, and I'm pleased you're in bed. You obeyed me, and that is what matters." He gave her a kiss, then reminded her to stay put, and limped out of the room.

Jacy leaned back against the pillows, prepared for another very long, boring evening. Wes couldn't have picked a punishment she would hate more than this one. It wouldn't even be a week until tomorrow night, and she honestly didn't know how she was going to get through this night after night for an entire month. She hated being alone and confined to the bed. It was impossible to sleep... and she wasn't permitted to read a book, or write in her journal. All she could do was lie here and stare at the ceiling or out the window, and wonder what was going on downstairs. For the umpteenth time since this started, Jacy wondered why Wes couldn't simply give her a severe switching and call it even. She would bear it gladly if it meant an escape from this hell.

****

The silence at the supper table got on Drew's nerves. Jolie was still sniffling, and pushing the food around on her plate, and Wes was angry and not talking to either of them. He tried again to get a decent conversation going, and when Jolie just looked at him mournfully, he got to his feet. "I think the two of you need to talk this out. I'm going to go in the other room."

"I don't have anything to say to Wes, other than I find him lower than a snake's belly!" Jolie announced, shooting to her feet and out the door in a flash.

Wes took another bite of the stew, and then looked at Drew, "Aren't you going outside and fetch her? Hell, she'll probably take off again."

"She's not leaving," Drew replied. "She's blaming herself that Jacy is in trouble... Feeling guilty because she knows that Jacy hates going to bed period, not to mention a good five hours earlier than normal every night."

"Maybe she should feel guilty," Wes commented, getting up and starting to clear the table. He'd washed up the dishes every night since sending Jacy to bed early.

"She was looking forward to seeing Jacy, and talking to her."

"They can talk in the morning."

Drew left the kitchen without another word.

****

Jolie found Jacy's garden and decided she would weed it for her. It wasn't something she enjoyed doing, but knew that Jacy probably hadn't had time to tend it properly. She slowly started making her way down the first row, and when she was finished, she started on the next one. She was so angry with

Wes that she simply didn't know what to do. And she couldn't understand why Drew didn't do something to help Jacy. Surely Wes would listen to him...?

It was all her fault, too. Poor Jacy was lying upstairs in a hot room, probably miserable, and thinking of all the things she could be doing... and it was her fault for leaving and upsetting Jacy. She wasn't the sort of woman who should go off riding the trail by herself. She wasn't very good with a gun, and she didn't even know how to use a knife. It terrified Jolie to think of her sister in the hands of the Comanche. And Wes probably felt the same way, which was why he was being so hard on her. Still, it wasn't fair... It just wasn't... and she had to do something to change Wes's mind.

Jolie was shocked when Wes joined her in the garden, and started pulling weeds.

"Jacy hasn't had much time to tend her garden this week," he said quietly. "I'm not trying to be mean to her, Jolie. I want to keep her safe, and her riding out of here after you was just plain foolish. She could have been killed."

"I imagine she knows that by now, Wes," Jolie said. "It's all my fault anyway... Please don't make her go to bed early any more. I promise I won't ride out again, and she'll not have a reason to come after me. I swear to that."

"Jacy promised me, too."

"Don't you believe her?"

"I do believe her. But, she has to be held accountable. I want her to have time to think about what it would have been like if that brave had carried her off and I couldn't find her. She would have spent the rest of her life regretting that impulse, Jolie... not just a few hours a night for a month. It may sound harsh to you, but it's nothing compared to what she would have gone through with them holding her captive... maybe torturing her, raping her." He picked a few more weeds, and then said, "I hate this, too. I'd rather have Jacy downstairs with all of us, happy and smiling, instead of upstairs crying."

Jolie was shocked to see him take a swipe at his eyes with his shirt sleeve, and she realized he was actually crying. "I wish you'd consider letting her off early, Wes. Or let me do it for her...?" she asked hopefully.

"You'd go to bed at six every night for the rest of her month?" Wes asked with a snort of disbelief.

"Yes, sir, I would... if you'd let her off."

Jolie was shocked when the man gave her a big hug. "Sorry, little sister, but I can't do it. Miss Jacy has to pay the price all on her own. You can help her best by encouraging her to behave herself and accept it as due."

****

Jolie finally stood and announced she was going to bed.

"You'd best not be planning to visit Jacy," Drew said quietly.

"What harm can it do?" Jolie whispered. "I just want to see for myself if she's okay."

Drew put down his book, stood, and took her arm. "Night, Wes," he called out, and then hurried his wife from the room and upstairs. He helped her gather her things from her old room and put them in his, and then picked up her hairbrush. "You come on over here," he patted the bed.

Jolie's eyes grew round, but she bravely walked over to stand in front of her husband. He pulled her down beside him, and to her surprise, he undid her braid, and then started brushing her hair. "Ummmmm," she purred contentedly. "This is nice."

"Much better to have this used on your hair than on your backside," Drew said pointedly. "Going into Jacy's room would earn you a spanking, little one, and knowing Wes, he'd probably tack a couple more days onto Jacy's punishment."

"That wouldn't be fair!" Jolie argued.

"It sure wouldn't be fair if you earned Jacy more punishment because you're upset with Wes..." Drew brushed her hair a few more strokes, then said, "Just try to be patient, honey. Wes loves Jacy with all his heart."

****

Wes shut the lights and went up to bed early. He wanted to be with Jacy. He entered the room quietly, just in case she was sleeping, and found her sobbing into her pillow. He moved to the bed, and took her in his arms, and rocked her back and forth, and finally she fell asleep in his arms. He gently lowered her head on the pillow, then undressed and crawled in beside her.

He lay awake for the next several hours, and when he did sleep, it was to have bad dreams. He was glad to see morning come.

"Why were you crying last night?" he asked Jacy when she was dressing.

She looked at him, and then said, "Because I miss you so much when I'm up here all alone. And because Jacy was home, and I couldn't see her either... and because I might never have had the chance to see any of you again... I kept thinking how awful it would have been..." She was on the verge of tears again, much to her dismay. "I'm sorry... I'm just being silly..."

"No, you're not being silly." He took her chin in his hand and turned her face up to his. "Have you learned your lesson, wife?"

"Yes, Wesley, I have. The thought of never seeing you or Drew or Jolie... I couldn't bear it at all... It's terrible for several hours a day, but it would be even worse if it was forever." Her lower lip started trembling, and she threw herself into his arms, crying again.

Wes held her and comforted her, then gave her a slap on the butt. "I'm hungry, Mrs. Parker! Feed me!"

Jacy hurried downstairs, and within minutes she had a nice breakfast on the stove. She took great delight in telling Jolie and Drew about the visit from Jacob and Lucy Fellows, and predictably, Jolie loved the idea of Mrs. Fellows getting her butt whipped out in the barn. Jolie told of their wedding, and about the bounty hunting, and about the bank robbery.

Wes was shocked, and didn't bother hiding it from his brother. "I can't believe she can sit down!" He looked back at Jolie, then said, "I'd spank you daily, girl, and keep you too sore to sit a saddle."

"Drew is smarter than that!" Jolie promptly replied, and had the satisfaction of seeing Wes turn red.

"I know a little lady who is asking for a good spanking," Drew warned, and when Jolie stuck her tongue out at him, he decided there was no time like the present.

Jolie tried to free herself from Drew's grasp, but she was unable to do so, and wearing the darn skirts kept her from fighting properly. The yards of material got in the way. Much too easily, he pulled her down across his knee, and his hard hand landed on the seat of her skirt with a whap.

"You need to settle down, Mrs. Parker," he advised her, willing to accept an apology if she offered one. "You've been needling Wes ever since we got home, and sassing me. It's going to stop right now, or this fanny is going to pay the price." He gave her another sound smack, and then asked, "Understand?"

Jolie was embarrassed at being turned over his knee in front of Wes and Jacy, and she wasn't going to give him the satisfaction of a reply.

Her silence earned her another smack, and a threat to toss up her skirts.

Wes got to his feet, trying not to grin, and took Jacy's hand. "Jacy and I are going down to the barn for a bit, bro. Feel free to show Jolie what happens to sassy little girls around here."

"Wes!" Jacy scolded.

"Come along, darlin', or I might start thinkin' you want a spankin', too," he teased.

Once she heard the kitchen door slam shut, Jolie tried to twist around to look at Drew. "I don't like being spanked in front of Wes and Jacy, Drew. It's embarrassing."

"Then don't act up in front of them," was his reply. "Are you going to settle now? Or do I need to find a bare fanny and turn it red?"

"I'll settle," Jolie decided, and was relieved when he released her.

"Next time, Jolie, I'll do it up proper."

****

Wes got a splinter in his finger, and went up to the house to get Jacy to take it out. As he reached the kitchen door, he could hear the sisters arguing.

"Why not? We could pull it off..."

"It wouldn't be right, Jolie. I know you mean well, but I just can't do it, no matter how tempting it sounds."

"It's all my fault, Jacy. Surely, I can lay there for a few hours while you weed in your garden. Drew won't come near the garden, and I know that Wes will be working on that corral again after supper. It would get you outside in the cool evening air, and..."

"And I know a young lady who needs a good switching," Wes stepped inside the door, a scowl on his face. "I expect you to march outside and tell Drew what you were up to, Jolie Parker. Right now!"

"It's not Jacy's fault, Wes. She said no. Please don't blame her..."

"You high tail it out that door before I forget you aren't mine to punish."

"She meant well, honey," Jacy defended her sister. "She knows that I'm going crazy up there every night."

"She's feeling guilty, and if my brother is as smart as I think he is, he'll deal with Jolie in a manner she won't much care for." He leaned down and kissed Jacy. "I'm proud of you for telling Jolie 'no', Jacy. If you'd agreed to her plan, we would have started the month all over again," he said clearly, his green eyes telling her that he was dead serious.

"Please don't think badly of Jolie, Wes. She's hurting and feeling guilty."

Wes nodded, "I know she is, and Drew will deal with it, I'm sure." He gave his Jacy another hug and kiss, then asked, "Darlin', could you get this splinter out of my finger?"

****

"Drew...?"

He looked up from the harness he was fixing. "Why the long face? You and Wes fussing again?"

"It's worse than that. I tried to talk Jacy into switching places with me tonight so that she could have some time outside. He overheard us talking. Please tell him that Jacy said 'no'. I don't want her to suffer because of me," Jolie insisted. "I didn't mean any harm... I just feel terrible that she's being punished, and it's all my fault!"

"Sounds to me like you've earned a good spanking."

Jolie bit her lower lip, and looked down at the ground. She'd known from the moment that Wes overheard them that

Drew would spank her... it was just a question of where and when and with what.

"We'll take care of the matter after supper tonight. You can go upstairs, and put on your nightdress, then wait for me in the corner of our room. Is that understood?"

"Yes, sir."

He sent her on her way, and Jolie decided that dreading a spanking was truly terrible. She would have several hours to think about it before it happened.

She went inside, and Wes was sitting at the table, and Jacy was pouring peroxide over his finger. "Did you talk to Drew?" he asked her.

"Yes."

"And?"

"He's going to spank me after supper tonight." There was no point in lying, because Drew would simply tell the truth.

"I imagine you'll feel better afterwards, little sister," the redhead told her with a trace of sympathy. "Don't you worry about Jacy. I won't ever punish her beyond what is needed and necessary. I love her too much for that." He gave her shoulder a comforting squeeze, and then went back to work.

"I'm sorry, Jolie. I didn't want you to get into trouble," Jacy poured coffee for both of them, then sat at the table with her twin.

"Wes didn't blame you, did he?" Jolie wanted to be sure.

"No, he didn't."

"You'd think he'd let you off early for refusing to switch places with me!" Jolie grumbled, and then looked at Jacy in surprise when she giggled. "What's so funny?"

"Oh, Jolie, you're still new to these Parker men. Once they make up their mind that it's for your own good, it's written in stone. Butting heads with Wes won't make a bit of difference. He's decided on a month, and it will be one month.

The best I can hope for as a reprieve is that he picks a thirty day month, and not one with thirty-one days!" She smiled at her sister, and then sighed. "Was Drew angry?"

****

"This is not fun," Wes grumbled, washing dishes. "I'll bet they did it on purpose, too."

"Of course they did it on purpose," Drew shook his head as he looked at the pile of dishes. "My little brat is going to get her butt tanned good."

"Give her at least a dozen for me," Wes said wistfully, and grinned when his brother chuckled. He ran a hand through his thick red hair, and then said, "I know she's mad at me, Drew, and I'm sorry it's making things tougher for you. This should be your honeymoon time, and Jolie's so caught up in punishing me for taking Jacy to task that she's ignoring you and acting up. I feel bad that you have to whip her butt right now."

"She's blaming herself and feeling guilty," Drew admitted. "The best thing I can do for her right now is give her something to think about. Maybe a few nights of going to bed early will settle her down."

"You'll end up hating it, too, and we'll be doing piles of dirty dishes every damn night until it's over," Wes reminded him. "And you know for a fact they'll dirty every last one they can, too."

"One way to stop that is to leave the dishes for them to do in the morning..." Drew said, waiting for Wes's inevitable reaction.

"Are you out of your mind? If Jacy got up and found this kitchen a mess, she'd bring the house down around me, and then she'd sneak down here in the middle of the night to clean. It's easier to do the dishes than have to spank her every damned night, and tack more time onto her punishment... Damn it, Drew... I want this over with!"

"You could give her some time off for refusing to listen to Jolie...?" Drew suggested, surprised his brother didn't think of that on his own.

Wes looked at him, then sheepishly admitted, "I intend to, brother, just as long as she continues to accept what she has coming for a bit longer."

Drew knew better than grin. One thing his brother hated was washing dishes. He'd bet anything that Wes would find several reasons to knock off some time and let his Jacy off early. In the meantime, he had his own sweet wife to deal with. He flipped Wes with the towel, and then said, "I need to go up and deal with Miss Jolie, brother. You've got this under control..." Listening to Wes sputter and call him names was the highlight of his day!

****

Jolie hated being in the corner, and she imagined her sister felt the same way confined to her bed. Jolie knew she deserved the spanking she was going to get. She shouldn't have tried to get Jacy to do something that would have earned her more punishment if she'd agreed. And, she had been terribly sassy with Drew, taking her temper with Wes out on her husband.

She heard the door open, and held her breath. The next few minutes were likely to be painful ones, and even though she knew she deserved a spanking, it didn't mean she was looking forward to it.

Drew walked over to the corner and said, "I see you're waiting where I told you to wait, honey, and that's good, but from now on, when you're sent to the corner, I want to see a bare butt on display. He gave her a solid spank, then said,

"Please pull up your gown, and keep your nose right where it is until I tell you otherwise."

It was impossible to believe that she could be any more embarrassed than she was already, but raising her nightdress and exposing her backside was all it took to cause her face to flood with color. Although they were married, and he'd made sweet love to her every night since they spoke their vows, she found it difficult to stand there exposed.

Drew was well aware that Jolie was finding it hard to stand there with her bare backside on display, and it pleased him to know that. He wanted her to feel very punished when he was through.

Jolie could feel Drew's dark eyes on her, and to her surprise, her eyes filled with tears.

****

Jacy was pretty sure she heard her brother-in-law go into his and Jolie's bedroom, and she wished she could do something to prevent what was going to happen. If she'd just stayed home in the first place... The door to the room opened suddenly, and she let out a small cry. She hadn't heard Wes come upstairs!

"I didn't mean to scare you!" he apologized at once. "Just checking to make sure you're being a good little girl," he added lightly. He could see the sheen of tears in her eyes and wished he could make her smile.

"If I'd stayed home in the first place, Jolie wouldn't be in trouble," she whispered.

"If Jolie'd stayed home in the first place, you wouldn't be in trouble, either. You both acted impulsively, and it affects the whole family when you do. Not another word, Jacy. You just spend this time wisely..." He left the room, and closed the door behind him.

****

"You can turn around now, Jolie, and tell me what you were thinking about."

Jolie looked at him. "I was thinking that it's hot up here!"

"It's going to get hotter for you in a few minutes," he refused to be baited. "What else were you thinking? And no more smart comments, please."

"I was thinking that if I'd stayed home, my sister wouldn't be going through hell every night. I hate this, Drew. I'd do anything to get her off the hook with Wes, but he won't hear of it! It's just not fair, and I don't know why he can't see that! It's my fault she rode out of here!"

"Jacy is a grown woman, honey. She made the choice to ride out, and it was a bad choice. She put her life in danger, and Wes has a right to punish her for doing so." He paused, and then added, "We're going to talk about your behavior. I agree. You chose to ride out of here on your own, and go after bounty. I let you off, and you turned right around the next day and chased outlaws. I don't think that spanking I gave you had much of an impression because you've been sassy ever since. I warned you to stop giving Wes a rough time, and you've persisted. You even tried to talk your sister into switching places with you. That is out and out defiance, Jolie. You disobeyed me, and you encouraged your sister to disobey her husband. What do you think we should do about this?"

Jolie looked at Drew in dismay. Surely he didn't expect her to answer that?

"I asked you a question, young lady."

"I don't know, Drew! You're the one who said I needed a spanking! I'm sure not going to give you any ideas!" she declared.

"You do need a spanking, a long hard spanking." He pulled a straight backed chair into the middle of the room, and then took a seat. "Come here, Jolie."

She gave him a dirty look, but walked over to stand in front of him. To her surprise, he grabbed her wrist and jerked her down over his lap. He started spanking her, fast and hard, and all she could do was squirm and yelp. The spanking went on and on, and finally she quit struggling and lay quietly, accepting the spanking.

"Do I have your attention now?" he wanted to know.

"Yes, sir," Jolie replied tearfully.

"Good. I asked you a question, and I expect an answer. What punishment do you deserve for your behavior?"

"This wasn't it?" she gasped.

"Nope. This was an attitude adjustment so we can talk. You still have a punishment coming to you, and I want to know what you think is fair."

"I'm not sure," she said truthfully.

"I'll give you some time to think about it." He helped her to her feet, and then sent her to the corner. "You have fifteen minutes to come up with something suitable, Jolie."

She stood there unmoving, wondering what he wanted her to say. She felt wretched, and wished she could undo the mess she created. The time passed before she could gather her thoughts, and she was stunned when he called her to come and stand before him.

"What did you decide?"

"I couldn't!" she admitted. "I'm just feeling terrible, Drew. Part of me wants to be mad at Wes, but it's really myself that I'm angry with. Jacy is nearly helpless, and when I think of her with that Comanche brave, it makes me ill. Wes should be upset with me, and not Jacy. If I'd been reasonable... but I'm not. I didn't want to go to Church, so I had a tantrum and rode out. I was scared, and didn't even try."

"Scared of what, honey? Mrs. Fellows?"

"Not of her, but of women like her. I don't want me to rub off on Jacy, and on you and Wes. My father was a drunk. He sobered up long enough to make a bounty, and then stayed drunk until the money ran out. I'm the one the minister stands up and condemns each week. I'm the one the ladies whisper about... I don't have polished manners like Jacy does. I'm not a lady, and I don't want Jacy cut off from her friends because of me! That's why I rode out." Jolie couldn't believe she'd admitted all of that, but there it was. And now Drew would despise her.

"Jolie, are you stupid?"

"No!" She was incensed.

"Are you able to learn new things?"

"Yes! Jacy's teaching me to write better, and to spell... Or she was until Wes stopped it!"

"Honey, Wes didn't stop the lessons. You and Jacy just need to take time during the day to work together. And you can learn anything you want to learn. You're intelligent, and beautiful. I'm not ashamed of you. In fact, I'm proud of you."

"You are?" her voice clearly said she didn't believe him.

"Yes, I am. Don't forget, honey. I know for an absolute fact you are a lady in every sense of the word. If you treat people well, they will treat you well. Your father isn't here, it's just you, and I will be proud to have you on my arm."

Jolie closed her eyes for a few seconds, trying to swallow over the lump in her throat. "Thank you," she finally whispered.

"I'm going to set your cute little butt on fire," he said softly. "You deserve it for giving Wes a rough time, and for sassing me. You also disobeyed me and interfered between Wes and Jacy. I won't permit that. I think a switching is what you deserve."

Jolie's eyes went wide. She'd expected him to use her hairbrush, or his belt... but not a switch! He held out his knife, and said, "Go and cut three switches, stand there and peel each one, then bring them up here."

"I'm not dressed!" Jolie pointed out.

"Wes won't bother you, young lady. And If I have to cut them, you won't be happy..."

Jolie reluctantly headed for the door, stopped and turned to face him. Whatever she was going to say died before she uttered a word, and she hurried to do as he bade.

****

Jacy spotted a movement outside in the yard, and she was shocked to see her sister running toward a tree. It was soon apparent that she'd been sent to cut a switch, and Jacy started crying. All Jolie was guilty of was wanting to help her out of the mess she'd gotten herself into. She turned over and cried in frustration. Life was so unfair at times.

****

Jolie cut the switches, and the longer she stood there peeling them, the more nervous she became. One switch was terrible, but three of them? Did he plan to use them all? She quickly weighed her options. He was upset over the way she'd acted toward Wes, and toward him, and that she'd come up with the plan to trade places with Jacy. He was going to give her three separate switchings!

The last time he'd taken a switch to her had been awful, and he'd given her twenty-five then, and that was for being rude to Lucy Fellows... This was much worse, and Jolie was starting to regret her actions big time!

****

    Drew watched from the window as Jolie took her own sweet time peeling the slender switches, and he couldn't help smiling. He wouldn't be in any hurry to feel their bite either. Finally, she started toward the house, and Drew made himself look as stern as possible. When he was done, Miss Jolie was going to feel well and truly punished.

Chapter Seven

Jolie dreaded opening the door to their room. She was scared spitless at the idea of a severe switching. Drew had already spanked her, and she was positive she was already red back there. The switch would be intolerable on her sore skin!

"Let me see them," Drew held out his hand, and then examined the three switches. "These will do nicely," he finally stated, picking one from the group and swishing it through the air. "We'll start with your temper toward Wes. He doesn't deserve it, Jolie. He's correcting his wife, and that is his right and his responsibility." He paused to let that sink in, and then pointed toward the chair. "Pull up your gown, and bend over and place your hands on the seat of the chair. I want your legs spread wide, too."

The look on Jolie's face was one of immense dread, and he'd been right to proceed in this fashion. She was already feeling punished, and it would go a long way toward easing her guilt.

"I'm going to give you ten," he said. "Do not move from your position, or we'll start over."

Jolie cried out when the switch left a line of scalding fire across her red bottom. The next line was across the base of her butt, and the next on her right thigh. Drew started at the top again, and this time ended with a stripe on her left thigh. "How many was that?" he asked.

"Six!" she hoped she was right.

"You have four more, and I'm going to give those on your thighs. Two to each side."

The anticipation was terrible, and it was all Jolie could do to stand there, knowing that the switch was going to bite her tender flesh. Drew was not gentle with her, and she knew the last four were the worst ones yet. She jumped when his hand rested on the small of her back.

"Will you apologize to Wes in the morning?"

"Yes, sir," Jolie agreed. She wasn't going to incur any more punishment over foolish pride.

"What will you say to him?"

Jolie stammered out a few words, and to her dismay, Drew wasn't satisfied. He switched her five more times, and then sent her to the corner to think of an appropriate apology. Five minutes later, he called her over to the chair again, and this time Jolie managed to offer an apology he found acceptable.

"Get back into position," he tapped her leg with the switch. "We'll deal with that sassy mouth of yours next. How many do you think you deserve?" he wanted to know.

Jolie thought for a moment then said, "Fifteen?"

"I agree," Drew nodded. He would have been satisfied with giving her ten, but if she was feeling that she deserved fifteen, he would give them to her. He kept most of them to her cheeks, and gave her a few on her thighs. She was crying when he finished, and hopping from foot to foot, but she hadn't moved her hands from the seat of the chair.

"What else are you to be punished for?" Drew wanted her to tell him.

"For trying to get Jacy to trade places with me..."

"For what it's worth, honey, I understand your feelings. But, it was wrong of you to ask Jacy to disobey Wes. Do you agree with that?"

"Yes, sir. I'm sorry... I just hate it that she's being punished because of me."

"You're feeling guilty as sin, and I think I have the cure for that," he promised her. "But first, we're going to make sure you won't try to talk Jacy into doing something like this again." He caught her left thigh, and then her right, and then moved up to her sit spot.

Jolie was miserable, and each new stripe felt as though it was on top of others, and it was. Drew landed a full dozen on the tender sit spot, and it was all she could do to accept them without raising up.

"We're done with this now, young lady," Drew said, walking over to the bed and turning down the covers. "I want you in bed right now, and you will retire with your sister for the next week. I think that sharing in her punishment will serve to make you think about the consequences of your actions the next time you are tempted to take off."

The look on Jolie's face was one of stunned surprise, but to her credit, she crawled into bed without a word. Drew leaned down and gave her a kiss, then left the room, leaving the switches laying on the chair in plain sight.

****

Not another word was said over the incident, and Wes accepted Jolie's apology the next morning with a big hug. Both women ate their supper early, and then went up to bed at the appointed time. If Drew expected Jolie to fuss over the punishment, he never let on, and Jolie didn't complain once. He suspected that she and Jacy commiserated with each other, but it was done when he and Wes were out of hearing.

"Is Jolie's time up now?" Wes asked as they rode out after breakfast to check on stock.

"Last night made a full week," Drew answered, suspecting his brother was planning to release Jacy, too.

They went in for the noon meal, and Wes looked at Jolie and asked, "Are you ever going to ride out of here again, Miss Jolie?"

"No!" she replied, surprised by his question.

"What about you, Miss Jacy? Have you learned your lesson?"

"I won't ever do that again, Wes. I already promised you..."

"Do you think that I should forgive the rest of the time you owe me?" he asked with a smile.

"I do!" Jolie promptly answered for her sister. "Wes, it's terrible going up there night after night, and having absolutely nothing to do for hours and hours."

"I know it's terrible, Jolie," he replied. "It's a punishment... and that is the whole point." He spoke to his wife again, "I'd like to let you off, honey, but you do not seem pleased by the idea...?"

"I'm just wondering if you're going to offer an alternative?" she admitted.

Wes chuckled, and then shook his head 'no'. "No, ma'am, no strings. If you are truly aware that what you did affected all of us, and that I expect it never to happen again, then I'd say the two weeks you spent going to bed early with your thoughts is ample."

Jacy smiled, then jumped up to come around the table and hug him. "Thank you, Wes!! Oh, thank you!"

"Just know that I'm not going to do any more dishes for a long, long time!" Wes grumbled. He caught the guilty look that flashed between the two women, and turned and winked at Drew. There was a time to be merciful…

The men rode out after lunch, and Jolie and Jacy decided it was time to beat rugs. Between the two of them, they pushed the furniture in the parlor aside, and carried the oval rug outside and hung it over the clothes line. Jolie went to work with the rug beater, and when she walked around to the other side, she was startled to find a painted Comanche brave standing there, his knife raised above his head.

Jolie was startled, and reached for her gun, which wasn't there! In the next moment she felt a blinding pain behind her ear, and she fell to the ground, unconscious. When she finally stirred, she wasn't sure how much time had passed. Her head was throbbing, but she managed to pull herself to her knees, and make it to her feet.

She suddenly remembered the Comanche, and gasped in horror as she thought of her sister. Where was Jacy? She called her name a few times, and searched everywhere, but there was no sign of her twin. She realized that he'd taken her sister captive.

Jolie tore off her clothes as she ran through the house, and within minutes she was on her horse, trailing them, and determined to get to Jacy before the brave could harm her in any way.

****

Drew cursed when he saw the note, and yelled for Wes.
Wes recognized the urgency in his older brother's voice, and came running. "What's wrong?" he demanded, then quickly scanned the note Drew held out. "Oh my God, no!"

"Jolie should have waited for us," Drew growled. "By now that Comanche probably has two captives!"

"I didn't think he would come this far, Drew," Wes said, his eyes full of anguish. "I should have killed him when I had the chance."

"You aren't a killer, Wes. We'll find them. We have to!"

****

Jacy was scared, and trying not to show any sign of weakness. As long as they were moving, the Comanche couldn't rape her. But, as long as they were moving, she was farther and farther away from home, and it would be hard for Wes to find her. She knew he would try, but this time the Comanche would be expecting him!

And Jolie! She couldn't believe she'd missed the brave and hit her own sister! While she was trying to see if Jolie was alright, he'd grabbed her and carried her off, and Jacy didn't struggle because she was afraid he'd kill Jolie if she did. She only hoped that Jolie would find Wes and Drew and have them come soon.

****

"Jolie is leaving us a marked trail!" Wes exclaimed.

"She's a smart one, but damn, I'm going to whip her butt for going off alone," Drew replied.

"I wonder why that Comanche took Jacy and not Jolie?" Wes questioned. "It doesn't make sense!"

"Maybe Jolie was in the outhouse, or inside, and Jacy was outside?"

"It's hard tellin' how much of a head start they have, Drew."

****

Jolie's head was throbbing mercilessly, and her stomach was nauseous. She felt like passing out cold, and it was sheer willpower that kept her tracking the Indian and her sister. The Comanche wasn't taking any pains to hide his trail, and that bothered Jolie. It meant that he was expecting to be followed, and wanted a confrontation. It also meant that he could be waiting behind every rock or tree that she passed. Jolie told herself that she needed to remain alert if she was to have a prayer of saving her sister.

She'd hoped that Drew and Wes would have caught up by now, but perhaps something had delayed them, and they didn't get home as soon as they expected. She heard something behind her, and whirled just in time to see an arrow coming straight at her.

****

Jacy tested her bonds, and couldn't move. She couldn't even cry out for help, because he'd gagged her before leaving her bound to the tree. She strained her ears, listening for every little sound, and constantly trying to loosen the rawhide strips around her wrists and ankles.

****

"He's leading Jolie on," Wes stated coldly. "Damn it, Drew. We've got to hurry the hell up or he's going to take her or kill her."

Drew didn't need any urging. He wanted his wife safe in his arms, and then he was going to whip her butt for scaring him half to death!

****

The arrow missed by an inch, and Jolie quickly pulled her gun and fired. The Comanche yelped, and Jolie knew she'd hit him. She could hear him moving, and trying to get away, and she gave chase. He suddenly appeared in front of her, knife drawn, and Jolie realized that her bullet had only grazed him. Just as he prepared to throw his knife, she shot again, and it was all over. Now all she had to do was find Jacy!

****

Drew and Wes looked at each other and rode as fast as they could. Gunfire could only mean one thing... Jolie was in trouble. A few minutes later they found the Comanche's body, but there was no sign of Jolie.

"I can't believe she shot him," Wes exclaimed.

"She's good with a gun, Wes," Drew wasn't surprised. He was too relieved that the body wasn't his wife's. "I just hope he was alone."

****

Jacy heard the shots, and was terrified. She was unable to call out for help, and had no way of knowing who fired the shots. She just knew that she'd been alone for over an hour now, and she would die unless she found a way to free herself.

An hour later, she was still struggling, when she heard someone approaching on horseback. She was sure it was the Comanche, and she prayed he wouldn't decide to attack her.

"Jacy!" Jolie said in relief when she spotted her sister. "Oh, Jacy!" She quickly dismounted and used her knife to cut her sister's bonds. "Are you alright?" she demanded, removing the gag.

"Thank God! We have to get out of here before he comes back, Jolie!" Jacy tried to get up.

"He won't be coming back," Jolie said quietly, and then got her canteen. "Here. You need to sip slowly so it doesn't make you sick."

Jacy relished every drop of water. "How on earth did you find me? Where are Wes and Drew? Taking care of the body?" she questioned.

"I left them a trail, but they aren't here yet."

"Oh my God... You found him, Jolie?"

Jolie nodded, her eyes full of tears. "We need to head home. I know the men will be worried."

****

Drew let out a sigh of relief when he spotted Jolie and Jacy coming toward them. Wes whooped, and rushed forward, anxious to hold Jacy. Drew took one good look at Jolie, and lifted her out of the saddle. "Are you hurt, honey?" he asked fearfully.

"What's wrong with Jolie?" Wes immediately demanded.

"She's really sick," Jacy explained. "I hit her..."

"You hit her?" two pairs of eyes looked at her accusingly.

"It was an accident," Jolie whispered. "Please don't talk loud."

"We were beating rugs, and the Comanche had a knife. He was going to kill Jolie, and I tried to hit his arm, but he moved back, and I hit Jolie on the head and knocked her unconscious. He grabbed me, and I didn't fight because I was afraid he'd kill Jolie!" Jacy started crying.

"Don't cry, sweetie," Drew told her kindly. "Jolie knows you weren't trying to hurt her." He looked at Jolie's head, and found a large knot behind her ear. It wasn't any wonder she had a headache. "I think we need to make a camp for the night," he told Wes. "Jolie needs to rest."

They made camp, and Jacy and Drew fussed over Jolie until she cried and just begged them to leave her alone. By morning her headache was all gone, and the foursome headed home, anxious to check on the livestock... and Jacy was worried about the parlor rug that was still hanging on the line.

"Are you upset with me, Drew?" Jolie looked over at him to inquire. He'd been so kind to her last night, but today she sensed he was very angry, and doing his best to hide it.

"You shouldn't have gone after Jacy alone, Jolie. I know you love her, but you could have been killed! It tears me up thinking of him attacking you!"

"I handled it, Drew," she said calmly. "I did what had to be done."

"It wasn't safe, Jolie," Wes added his two cents worth. "I love Jacy with all my heart, but honey, you should have waited for us."

"You two are so aggravating. Of the three of us, I'm the one most qualified to deal with a situation like this!!! You just don't like being shown up by a woman!" she added, then wished she could take back the words.

"That was uncalled for, wife, and it will be dealt with."

"No, Drew!" Jacy pleaded for her sister. "Jolie didn't mean it."

"Then she shouldn't have said it."

"Well, I can tell you right now, I would have gone after Jolie if the situation were reversed!!!" Jacy bravely declared.

"And I'm thinking you just might be wantin' a spankin', too, young lady," Wes growled at his wife.

"Wesley!" Jacy wailed.

"Forget it, Jacy. Their pride is smarting right now..." Jolie glared at the men, and then decided to keep quiet. There was no point in making matters worse.

By noon, Drew noticed that Jolie was having a difficult time. "Your headache is back, isn't it, honey?" he reached over to touch her arm, then felt all traces of his earlier irritation fall away as she turned pain-filled eyes on him and nodded. "We'll stop for a bit so you can rest." He rode ahead to speak to Wes, and they stopped.

Jacy quickly made a bed for her sister, and helped her to sip some water. "You just try to close your eyes and sleep for a bit..." When Jolie did as she was told without protest, Jacy whispered to Drew, "I'm really worried about her, Drew. She needs a Doctor."

Wes nodded in agreement, and then said, "Why don't I ride ahead, take care of the stock, and go into town and get Doc to come out to the house. You should be home by then, and he can give Jolie a once over."

"Sounds like a good idea," Drew replied, relieved that Wes was going to get the Doctor for Jolie.

"Jacy, you stay with Drew, and I'll see you tonight..." Wes gave her a kiss, and then he pulled her close and hugged her tight. "I mean it... don't you dare get taken away from me again!"

"I won't!" Jacy promised solemnly.

"I'll keep her safe, little brother," Drew patted his shoulder comfortingly.

"I'm counting on it." Wes mounted, and hurried off.

When Jolie woke up, her headache had diminished somewhat and she insisted they start for home again. "Where's Wes?" she wanted to know, and her eyes went wide when Drew told her he'd gone for the Doctor. "I don't want to see a Doctor!" she insisted. "I'm fine!"

"You are not fine, Jolie," Jacy said gently. "You're having terrible headaches, and it's all my fault!"

"No it's not!" Jolie insisted, and then looked at Drew. "I don't want to see a Doctor, Drew. Please!"

"There's no need to fuss over it, honey. You're going to be examined, and that's that."

"No, I am not!" she stubbornly refused. "You can't make me!"

Drew decided not to argue with her. "If it comes to that, honey, I can and will. Now stop fussing at me and concentrate on riding before you fall off your horse."

Jolie was insulted by his words. She'd never fallen off a horse in her entire life! And she wasn't going to see any ole Doctor either! She'd never been to one in her life, and she wasn't going to start now!

Drew insisted they stop once more for Jolie to rest a bit, and when she fussed at him, he merely lifted her from her saddle and smacked her bottom a couple times for her efforts. She teared up instantly, and then agreed to rest for just a couple minutes. An hour later, she woke again, and Drew insisted she ride with him. He didn't like the fact that she was obviously still in a lot of pain.

Once the ranch was in site, Jolie tried to sit up and smile and pretend she was fine. "I'm feeling great now, Drew," she fibbed. "You can just send that Doctor right back to town."

"Jolie, you're going to let the Doctor examine you, and that is final."

"Oh no I'm not!" she yelled, then jumped off the horse and took off running...

"Jolie Parker, you come right back here!" Drew growled. When she didn't listen, he jumped off his horse and gave chase. A few minutes later he was wishing he'd stayed on his horse!! The little blonde could run like the wind.

Jolie turned to look over her shoulder, and that was her undoing. One minute she was running along just fine, and in the next, the toe of her boot connected with a rock, and she went flying through the air to land in a breathless heap on the ground. She struggled to get up, but couldn't... and Drew had her!

"Are you hurt?" he asked angrily, feeling her legs and arms to see if she'd broken anything. "I swear, little girl, I'm going to whip your butt until it's beet red!"

"You just... try... it and.... I'll... give.... you what... for...!" Jolie gasped for air.

"Okay," he agreed, then calmly flipped her over and smacked the seat of her pants.

"Ow! No!" Jolie yelped. "Please... I... can't... breathe...!"

Drew stopped immediately, stood up, and picked her up to carry her back to the house. "You are going to see the Doctor, Jolie Parker. You are going to cooperate. You are going to be a good little girl. If you so much as look at the man cross-eyed, I am going to bare your fanny, and spank it right there in front of him, and THEN you will be seen and you will cooperate. And, don't think I'm going to let you off the hook, either. You've got a good hiding coming to you just as soon as I'm sure you're up to it."

"I don't want to see a Doctor, Drew!!! Please...!" Jolie started struggling with him.

"Jolie, what the hell is wrong with you?" he was having a rough time holding onto the spirited little blond. "Stop wiggling, damn it!" he found himself sitting on the ground to hold her. "That tears it... You have gone too damned far!" He managed to twist her struggling form down over his knee, and in the next instant, he started spanking her hard."

Jolie started crying. Her head was aching so much she could barely see straight, and the spanking hurt. She went limp simply because she had no fight left in her. "Please, I'm going to be sick..." she whimpered, and to her shame, she started retching.

Drew felt guilty as hell, and did his best to help her. "Damn it, honey... Stop fighting me. You're sick...!" He wiped her face the best he could, then picked her up again and headed for the house. She's stopped fighting, and was crying silently.

Jacy was waiting for them, a worried expression on her face. "Wes isn't here with the Doctor yet. Let's get Jolie into bed."

"She needs cleaned up, Jacy. She got sick..."

"Oh no!"

Jolie hated having the two of them fussing over her, but she didn't have a bit of strength left to protest. She found herself stripped out of her trail clothes, bathed, dressed in a gown, and tucked into bed. She closed her eyes, and went to sleep, praying they would just leave her alone to die in peace.

"Okay..." Drew looked at his angry sister-in-law. "You can tell me what a jerk I am, Jacy."

"You are just as bad as your brother, Andrew Parker!" Jacy didn't need a second invitation. "How could you spank Jolie when she is that sick?"

"She was fighting me, and I lost my damned temper. I'm not proud of myself, either," he mumbled darkly.

"You need your butt kicked!" Jacy scolded. "She's so sick she doesn't know what she's doing..."

"I know, Jacy," he admitted sheepishly.

"You just better behave yourself, Mister... or else!" Jacy threatened just as Wes walked in the door with the Doctor.

"Jacy Parker, what's gotten into you?" Wes scolded.

"It's okay, Wes. I had it coming," Drew gave his brother a meaningful look. "Glad you could come, Doc. My wife isn't feeling good at all."

"Well, take me to her and let's get her fixed up," the man said with a cheerful smile.

Drew led the way, and walked into the bedroom just in time to see Jolie climbing out the window. He rushed across the room, and grabbed her before she could swing out onto the tree limb she had hold of. His guilty conscience and remorse for his earlier treatment of her was forgotten in the space of two seconds flat, and replaced with indignation. "Are you trying to kill yourself, little girl?" he demanded.

"You let go of me, Drew Parker. I'm not going to see any ole Doctor and you can't make me!" she screeched.

"The hell I can't!" Drew argued, "I'm going to toast your backside until you settle down!" he promised, and then glared at the others. "OUT!"

"Drew, don't you dare!" Jacy started forward, only to have her husband grab her from behind and lift her off her feet.

"You are going to butt out of this, Mrs. Parker," he whispered.

"I am not going to let him spank Jolie again, Wes!" Jacy dared to argue with her husband, and then started kicking him in the shin to get him to release her.

"Hold on here!" the Doctor raised his voice above the din. "Just hold on... all of you! Wes, you and Jacy go on downstairs and put on some coffee. Jacy, I'm not going to let Drew spank this pretty sister of yours... at least not until I get a look at her. You behave now, and find me something to eat, you here?"

Jacy nodded, and then gave Drew a heated look before she flounced out of the room.

"Wes, take it easy on Jacy... She's not to blame for this," Drew cautioned his brother.

"I'm not going to put up with tantrums, Drew. Jacy knows better."

"Not now, Wes," the Doctor ordered, then pointed to the door. Once it closed behind Wes, he looked at Jolie. "All right, young lady, just what have you got against Doctors?"

Jolie just glared at the Doctor and refused to speak.

"Jolie, what is wrong with you?" Drew was exasperated and honestly didn't know what to do with her. "Honey, you need to let Doc look at you and help you."

"I'm fine," she insisted.

"You don't look fine, young lady," the Doctor crossed the room to stand beside the chair where Drew held her. "You're in pain."

"I'm fine!"

"Jolie, I'm going to spank you!" Drew threatened, and no one in the room was stupid enough to think he didn't mean it.

"There's not going to be any spanking, young man, not until I say so, anyway. Are you scared of doctor's, honey?" he asked kindly.

"She's never seen one before, Doc," Drew answered for her.

"I know what they do... and that is bury people!" she declared. "I'm not dying!"

"Well, no, you surely aren't dying," Doc chuckled. "Anyone who can climb out of bed and out a window isn't dying..." He shook his head. "I do treat people who aren't dying, Jolie. I give them medicine, try to make them feel better."

"Everyone I ever knew who went to a doctor died right away!" she argued.

"Were they old?"

"Not all of them..."

"Young people get sick too..."

"This one was shot. Went to get patched up, and died instead."

"I see. Well, Jolie, I haven't had anyone die on me for a long while. I like to keep my patients healthy. I just want to look at you, check you out, and I won't do anything without telling you first... agreed?"

"She agrees," Drew stated firmly.

"I didn't ask you, I asked Jolie."

Jolie giggled at Drew's expression. "Okay... As long as you promise...?"

"I promise, honey," he said solemnly.

Jolie looked him in the eye for a few long moments, and then nodded her agreement. "I'll trust you this once... since it will make Drew happy..."

"Thank you, Jolie," the Doctor replied with a smile for her, then got down to business before she changed her mind again. "Wes said you got smacked on the head. Where at?"

Jolie showed him, and he took a good look. "Still a bit swollen, but it's nothing that serious... Where are your headaches?"

Jolie answered all his questions, and then smiled when he told Drew to put her to bed to let her sleep it off. "I'm going to give you a powder to help with the pain... and leave another for tomorrow if you aren't all better. Think you just have a bad headache, honey, and sleep will help it more than anything... and maybe a cup of good tea..."

Jolie watched as he mixed the powder into a glass of water, then she drank it all down under their supervision. Drew put her into bed, and pulled the sheet and blanket up to cover her.

"That wasn't so awful, was it, Jolie?" Doc asked with a gentle smile.

"No... I'm sorry I was such a baby..." she said by way of apology. "You were nice to me..."

"You were brave to put aside your fear... You rest now, and I'll be by tomorrow to check on you..."

"I'll come up and check on you in a bit, honey," Drew promised, then followed the Doctor downstairs and to the kitchen.

"How is Jolie, Doc?" Wes demanded with a worried frown.

"She's got a bad headache, what is called a migraine headache," Doc replied.

"Did I do that to her?" Jacy asked tearfully.

"It might have triggered it, but I suspect it was worry for your safety that made it worse. She needs to rest and sleep it off. Should be better tomorrow," he answered. "Are you all right, Jacy? That buck didn't harm you, did he?" he demanded, his voice gruff with concern.

"I'm fine. My wrists are a bit tender where he tied me, but Jolie saved me from him," she answered.

"Good. Now where's my food?" he grinned.

****

Drew went upstairs right after the Doctor left, stating he wanted to keep an eye on Jolie.

Wes waited until he was out of earshot, and then said, "I think we'll take care of that spankin' you've earned right now, young lady."

"Drew deserved a scolding!" Jacy argued, putting her hands on her hips to glare at the tall redhead.

"Maybe he did, Mrs. Parker, but I won't have you interfering between him and Jolie. We've had this discussion before... and when I tried to calm you upstairs, you kicked me. When have I ever permitted you to throw a tantrum and get away with it?"

She looked at him for a few seconds, and then replied in a small voice, "Never..."

"And I'm not going to let it pass this time either," Wes announced. "You can bring me the wooden spoon, Jacy, and we'll get this spankin' started."

Jacy stomped over to the cupboard, opened a drawer, and removed a wooden spoon. When she turned around, Wes looked at her, and then raised one eyebrow in arch disapproval.

"That one would snap in two the first time I spanked you with it. I want the heavy spoon, Jacy, and you will get twenty-five extra with it for trying to pass off the other one."

Jacy got the spoon he wanted, then gave the drawer a violent shove, making the whole cupboard shake, and an empty pie tin fall on the floor.

"Pick that up!" Wes growled menacingly. She slammed it on the work surface of the cabinet, and he shook his head. "Bring the spoon to me, woman."

Jacy handed it to him with a snap, her blue eyes flashing in temper.

"You can take yourself over to that corner, raise your skirts, and push your drawers down to your knees, Miss Jacy. You've turned a simple spankin' into a serious punishment now. Your attitude has earned you a good strappin'."

"No!" Jacy paled. "I didn't mean it... It's just that you always take Drew's side with everything!"

"This isn't about Drew, Jacy. This is about the fact you kicked me while having a temper tantrum... and now it's about your attitude and more temper... You have five seconds to have your nose in that corner with your bare butt peeking at me... or I'm going to take you outside and cut a switch!"

Jacy immediately headed for the corner. She faced it as she fumbled with her skirts and lowered her drawers to her knees. "What if Drew comes down?" she asked in embarrassment.

"Then he'll see my naughty wife with her nose in the corner waiting for a spankin'," Wes replied. "I want you to think about your attitude, darlin'. I warned you early on that I wouldn't put up with nonsense..."

"I'm sorry," she whispered contritely. "Please, Wes... It's been a rough couple of days..." she whined.

"Stop making excuses for bad behavior. I won't listen to them, and I won't let you justify your temper tantrums and attitude. You be quiet now and keep your nose in that corner until I call you for your spankin'. Keep that skirt pulled up, too. I want to see that butt of yours..."

****

Drew was relieved to see that Jolie was sleeping peacefully. She'd scared him when she got sick all over him after she ran from him. Doc said that was a fairly normal occurrence with these serious headaches... But, he was determined she was going to stay in bed until Doc came and pronounced her fit again. Then he was going to put her over his knee and warm her backside proper.

She'd risked her life! And he wanted her to make a better choice if something like this ever happened again. She should have waited for him and Wes to come home... Both she and Jacy could have been raped or killed... She was brave, and damn good with a gun, but she was his wife now, and he would protect her... from herself if necessary. And, he rubbed one of the spots where she'd fought him, she was going to learn to control her temper and talk to her husband when she was scared or upset about something.

Drew decided he needed a cup of coffee, and headed downstairs. He stopped just short of the kitchen when he spotted his brother sitting there holding a wooden spoon and twirling it between his fingers. It didn't take much deductive reasoning to realize that little Jacy was in for a session over Wes's knee, just by the set of Wes's jaw. He hoped like hell that it didn't have anything to do with him, and then decided he didn't need a cup of coffee right now. Poor Jacy was probably standing in the corner with her bottom bared... and he wouldn't humiliate her by setting foot in the kitchen. He quietly turned and headed back upstairs...

"Okay, Jacy, let's try this spankin' again. You come on over here now, and lay over my knee."

Jacy was hopeful that Wes would forget the strapping if she cooperated. She walked to him, and put herself over his lap, turning her bottom up, and making sure her skirts were out of the way. "I'm sorry for my temper and attitude, honey. I should have accepted the spanking without a fuss," she said contritely.

"Yes, you should have. Now you're in for a real good tannin'," Wes stated, fully aware that she was trying to mitigate her punishment, and not about to let her off easy. If he did, she'd just push him harder and further the next time.

Jacy was surprised when Wes started spanking her, using his hand. The spanks weren't especially severe, but they did sting. He made sure to turn her cheeks a nice shade of pink, then spanked her thighs so that they matched her bottom.

Wes picked up the spoon, and gave her a light spanking with it, covering her bottom and her thighs, then he stopped, and said, "That was the spankin' you were goin' to get, Jacy. Was it worth the tantrum you had over it?"

"No, sir. I'm sorry, and I will do better," she replied immediately. "May I please get up now and go see to Jolie?"

"I said that was the spankin' you were goin' to get... You earned another twenty-five with the spoon for getting out that little puny one..."

Jacy gasped when the spoon cracked with a vengeance on her sit spot again and again. "Ouch! Ohhhhhhhhhh! Owwwwwwwwwwwwwwwww! Please, Wes... Stop!!! I'm sorrrryyyyy!" she wailed.

Wes cracked her again, this time on the top of her right thigh. "Doesn't seem so funny now, does it, Jacy?" He continued to spank her thighs... then moved up to her bottom, ignoring her cries of pain and making the spanks felt.

"OWWWWWWWWW! Wesley, please.... No more... No more....!"

"That was twenty-five..." he told her, and grinned when she stopped kicking and relaxed. "We could have stopped right here," he told her, "but what did you do next? Slammed the drawer, knocked off the pie tin, slammed it down on the table when I told you to pick it up, and then you slapped my hand with the spoon when you handed it to me.... Do you expect me to let you off after acting like a spoiled brat having a tantrum?"

"Oh, Wes... Please... I'm sorry! I didn't mean any of it... honestly... Please don't use your belt...!" she begged.

"Would you rather cut a switch?" he asked.

"No!!!! I don't need any more spanking, I swear I don't! I'm sorry, honey...."

"And you will be even sorrier in a little while," he told her, lifting her to her feet. "You just go and put your pretty little nose in that corner and think about your actions. I want you to come up with a number for me..."

"Wes, I hate it when you ask me to do that!" she cried, but she was on her way to the corner.

"I hate it when you act like a spoiled brat," he told her. "Think of a number, Jacy, and be fair," he warned her.

How did she know what he thought was fair? Her poor bottom was stinging already, and the belt on top of it wasn't going to be pleasant. What would he think fair? Was five enough? Or maybe six? She hated it when Wes made her tell him what she thought was fair. If she said too few, he would tell her she wasn't taking it seriously enough, and would very well add another spanking at bedtime... If she said too many, he would assume she was feeling guilty and needed every last stroke to make her feel better. There was no winning... and Jacy wasn't going to do it this time! He could do what he wanted, but she'd be damned if she'd give him any numbers!

Chapter Eight

The minutes ticked by slowly, and Wes watched and waited. He knew that if he pulled Jacy out of the corner too soon, he was going to have to give her a sound whipping because she was going to be sassy. She needed time to get past her stubbornness and decide to cooperate and give him a number. She was going to take her medicine whether she wanted to or not.

Jacy started getting nervous. The longer she waited, the worse the anticipation. She didn't want a strapping... It hurt so much, and usually left welts that burned for a good long while, and made sitting difficult. She shouldn't have slammed the drawer. She knew it would upset Wes... and slamming down the pie tin was another thing she shouldn't have done... and why on earth had she slapped the palm of his hand with the bowl of the wooden spoon? Did she have a death wish?

She didn't have a number in mind... but was certain that Wes did. She just wanted it over with... She hated standing in the corner...

"Do you have a number yet, Jacy?" Wes asked.

"No..." she admitted.

"Why not?"

"I don't know what you consider fair... Please don't make me guess..."

"Sorry, you bought the spankin'. What is fair? I want a number."

"Okay... five!" she declared.

"I don't think you've stood there long enough yet," Wes scolded. "You had a major temper tantrum. Slammed a drawer, knocked a pie tin on the floor. Then picked it up and slammed it down on the table... then you slapped me with the wooden spoon... You think five is a reasonable punishment for showin' me disrespect?"

"One for slamming the drawer... two for the pie tin... and three for smacking your hand with the spoon," she explained.

"Smackin' my hand with the spoon is grounds for a punishment all by itself. I was tryin' to give you a chance to show you knew you behaved badly, Jacy."

"I do know that... but I had a right to be upset!" she insisted.

"You had a right to have a temper tantrum and kick me, then throw a major fit when I told you that you were goin' to get a spankin' for it? Sorry, darlin', I won't let you act like a brat. I'll give you five more minutes to think about this, and then we're goin' to get real serious."

Jacy stomped her foot. She just couldn't resist. Damn, Wesley Parker was the most aggravating stubborn man who lived! She wasn't going to give him the satisfaction of changing her number. It was more than fair. She didn't even think she deserved five!!!

"Well, Jacy? How many?"

"I was being generous, Wes. I don't think I deserve any!" she declared. "I'm through with this! I'm going to go upstairs and check on Jolie, and if you don't like it, then too damn bad!" She dropped her skirts and headed for the doorway.

****

"Hey there... You don't have to sit here, Drew. I'm feeling lots better," Jolie said with a smile.

"You haven't slept long," he frowned.

"I felt your eyes on me," she grinned. "I'm okay, honest. You can go and help Wes... If I need anything I'll call Jacy."

"You sure?" he wanted to know.

"Positive. I'm going to stay right here and sleep. My head feels a lot better now, and I want it to stay that way."

"I do too," he leaned over and kissed her gently.

"Are you still going to spank me for going after Jacy by myself and not waiting for you and Wes?" she asked with her eyes closed.

"You bet I am," he didn't lie to her.

"She's my sister, you know. I had to go. It's the way I am. I'm not someone to sit and wait for a man to take charge."

"And I'm not one to let my wife risk her life and not take her to task for it."

She smiled, "I love you, you know."

"I love you too, Jolie," he answered, then smiled when she softly snored. He gave her another kiss, and then headed for the door.

He hoped like heck that Wes was done with Jacy so he could get a cup of coffee. He started downstairs, and was headed for the kitchen, when Jacy came flying around the corner and ran straight into him. He grabbed her arms to steady her and keep her from falling, and winced when she kicked him hard! "What the heck..." he growled.

"Let me go!" she whispered frantically, but before Drew could do so, Wes was right there, and had Jacy in a firm grip.

"That little piece of foolishness has moved this out to the barn…" He picked her up with one strong arm around her waist, and headed through the kitchen, and out the back door.

Drew couldn't help smiling as he spotted a pair of very feminine drawers dangling from the toe of Jacy's shoe. If he was a betting man, she would be more embarrassed about that than she would be at the spankin' her husband was about to give her.

He went to the stove and poured himself a cup of coffee, then sat down at the table to enjoy it, his mind imagining the scene in the barn. He didn't envy his brother the job, and didn't blame him a bit for dealing with Jacy's temper. He was planning to do the same with his half of the twins just as soon as Doc gave him the okay…

****

"Wesley Parker, you just put me down right now!" Jacy screeched. He ignored her, of course, and she continued to bump against his side as he carried her like a valise, his strong right arm wrapped around her tiny waist.

Wes headed straight for the barn, and dumped Jacy on a bench just inside the door. She tried to scramble to her feet, but he simply grabbed her arms and sat her down with a thump.

"Owww! Wes! That hurts! You spanked me already, remember?" she tried to reach back to rub the injured spot.

"I'm goin' to spank you again," he told her. "What's gotten into you, Jacy Parker? You know better than to act like that? Kickin' Drew, swearin'? You've earned yourself a good tannin', and I'm goin' to see you get one."

Jacy didn't have time to protest. He pulled her up from the bench, and sat down himself, then jerked her down over his lap. In the next instant her skirts were flipped up, and his hard hand found her bared backside. The spanks were damned hard, and she knew she'd pushed Wes past his tolerance level. "Owwww!" she squealed and kicked. "No more, please! I'm sorry!"

"I haven't even started," he told her. "You aren't goin' to be able to sit down without feelin' this spankin' for at least a week!" he promised.

Jacy was positive he meant each and every word, and was pretty sure she was already reaching the 'can't sit' state! "I'm sorry! Please stop, Wesley. I'll be good now... Please... No more... I'm so sore already!!! Ohhhhhhh! Stop!" she bawled.

Wes ignored her. He spanked her cute little bottom and upper thighs until his hand was stinging unbearably, and then he reached behind him and took down a leather strap that had only one purpose... spanking his wife's backside when she went too damned far!

Jacy let out a yelp of pained surprise when the strap landed on her reddened cheeks. "Oh no, Wes... Please...!" The leather strap was by far worse than his belt. He rarely used it, and when he did, it was a memorable occasion. She was crushed. "Please, don't, honey! I'm so sorry! I apologize. Please don't use that strap... It's awful..."

"You're behavior was awful." He gave her another hard lick, and watched the welt appear almost instantly.

Jacy screamed. "I can't bear this, Wes! I thought you loved me?!"

"I love you too much to let you get away with actin' like that!" he countered. "You earned this lickin', Jacy, so just lie here and take it." He walloped her again, this time on her thighs, and her scream was even louder. Her sensitive sit spot was next to receive a blow, and he wasn't surprised when she moaned and collapsed across his lap. The strap was merciless... and she was already sore. "Are you goin' to throw a tantrum the next time I tell you to come to me for a spankin'?" he demanded, giving her another hard stripe in the same exact spot.

Jacy was sobbing so hard she could barely talk. "I won't," she finally promised.

"And when I tell you to give me a number, are you goin' to throw a fit, and run off?"

The hard leather strap landed a third time on her sit spot, and she stiffened, then whispered, "No, no, no, no, no...."

Wes knew she'd had enough. "Very well. You go on up to the house, take yourself upstairs to our room, and stay there. You are not comin' downstairs again until you come up with a fair number for the tantrum you threw, and you answer for it. I'll be up in an hour or two to see if you're in a more reasonable frame of mind. If you aren't, we'll be makin' another trip out here for another round with this strap." He slapped her sore bottom once more with his hand, and then put her on her feet.

Jacy was scandalized when she saw her drawers lying on the ground by the kitchen door. She scooped them up in one hand, and then raced through the kitchen without glancing in Drew's direction.

Drew could hear her crying as she ran up the stairs, and he turned his dark eyes toward his brother. "What on earth did the wee one do?" he couldn't help asking.

"I was goin' to give her a little spankin' for that temper tantrum she had in front of Doc, and she had to go and make a big fuss over it. Lord that woman has a temper at times." Wes commented, helping himself to a cup of coffee, joining his brother at the table, and rubbing his hand. "I hope her butt hurts as much as my hand does!" he grumbled.

"You used that leather strap on her, didn't you? Guess her butt hurts a whole lot worse than your hand," Drew said dryly.

"Worst part is I still owe her a strapping with my belt for the tantrum she had in here," Wes said glumly.

"I owe Jolie one, too," Drew said quietly, and then looked at his brother. "I don't want to do it, though."

"Nope, don't reckon you do. She probably saved Jacy. Kept that brave movin' so he didn't have time to hurt her... but she risked her fool neck, too. She's lucky she didn't get taken, too, Drew. I know you don't want to whip her fanny, but if it was me, I'd do the same."

****

Jacy was miserable, and threw herself face-down on the bed to have a good cry. At least he hadn't told her to stand in the corner!

Her poor bottom was in some serious pain now, and Wes wouldn't be satisfied until he took his belt to her for her earlier behavior. She simply didn't know what she could do to convince him she was truly sorry... and didn't know why she'd behaved so badly. She pondered the question, and tried to settle on a number that would be fair.

When Wes opened the door to their room a good two hours later, he found her sleeping. He could tell she'd been crying. Her cheeks were red, and streaked with her tears. He felt bad, but was determined to let Jacy know he wasn't going to permit her to behave like a spoiled brat. He leaned down and stroked one cheek, and woke her.

Jacy smiled at her husband, and then remembered that she was in trouble, and that he was here to give her another whipping. Her blue eyes promptly filled with tears. "I'm sorry, Wes. I know I was awful earlier... and I have no idea why."

"I believe you, honey," he said gently.

"You do?" she asked hopefully.

"I do believe you, but I'm not goin' to let you off the hook. Your behavior brought on everythin' extra that's happened today. One simple spankin' turned into a battle of wills... and we aren't startin' with that."

"I would take that spanking in a heartbeat if you gave me the chance to do it all over," she told him sincerely. "I'm truly sorry, Wes... I won't act like that again," she promised.

"I sure hope you don't," he replied. "Have you come up with a fair number?" he asked her.

"No... I fell asleep without deciding on anything," she admitted. "I think the worst thing I did was slapping your hand with the spoon... It was disrespectful. Slamming the drawer and the pie tin... Well, those were just temper... and frustration... I don't think they warrant serious punishment... maybe five for them together...?" she asked timidly, looking at him for approval.

"Five will settle for those," Wes agreed. "How many more for the spoon?" he wanted to know.

"Twenty?" she asked.

"Is that all?" he asked.

"It wasn't a conscious, deliberate act... It was done in temper, Wes... and I do regret it very much..." she explained.

"You're makin' excuses," he scolded gently. "Disrespect is disrespect, and it doesn't matter if it's part of a temper tantrum or not. You can be angry, and still be respectful," he argued his point.

"Yes, sir, I apologize."

"Does that change your number?" he wanted to know.

Wes wasn't going to be satisfied until she expressed the proper amount of regret for her tantrum, and Jacy knew that prolonging the discussion was going to make the reckoning even more painful. She took a deep breath, and then let it out slowly, whispering, "Thirty-five would be more appropriate."

"Yes, it would, and five more for the slamming..." Wes looked down at her, and then said firmly, "I want you to arrange the pillows on the bed, Jacy, and take off your clothes. I want you completely bare, and your butt up over the pillows, legs spread wide."

Jacy was positive it would do no good to argue with her husband. If she did, he would probably add additional punishment, and she was too sore to contemplate such a terrible thing.

She scooted off the bed on her tummy, and then piled the pillows, putting off undressing as long as possible. She'd dressed and undressed in front of her husband countless times, but it was embarrassing to take off her clothing so that he could punish her.

Wes waited patiently. Jacy normally tried to plead with him to permit her to leave on everything but her skirts and drawers, her logic that he wasn't spanking her anywhere else but her backside, so why did she need to undress completely? Today, however, she undressed without an argument, then climbed on the bed and put herself in position.

Wes could immediately see why she was being so cooperative. Her butt and thighs were bruised and welted, and getting another spanking on top of them was going to be extremely painful.

Jacy was waiting for Wes to take off his belt, and praying he wouldn't be too harsh with her. She had no idea how she would remain in place as it was.

"Your butt looks sore, wife," Wes commented.

"It is sore... very sore," she agreed. "I don't know if I can stay in place," she admitted, "and I don't want to earn extras... Could you hold me just this once?" she asked hopefully.

"Part of the punishment is staying in place for it, Jacy, you know that," he said mildly. "It shows me that you accept the fact you were wrong and you deserve the correction."

"I know... and I do... honestly... It's just that I already hurt so much, Wes... I don't know if I can do it..."

"Jacy, honey, you don't know how much I want to let you off right now... Take you in my arms, comfort you, and just forget this whippin'... but I can't do that," he said regretfully. "You brought this all on yourself, and you've no one but yourself to blame for the consequences. I'm goin' to give you a good lickin', and hope you never need to have this lesson repeated."

Jacy heard the sound she'd been dreading... Wes unbuckled his belt and pulled it through the loops on his pants, doubled it, then slapped it against his hand. It was a sound that never failed to set her stomach on edge and cause her to squirm in anticipation of the belt's bite. That anticipation was even more fearful today... because she knew she would never be able to stay in place... she was in too much pain!

****

Jolie woke again, feeling even better than before. She discovered she was hungry, and decided she was going down to the kitchen and find something to eat. She put her wrapper on over her nightdress, and took a minute to run a brush through her hair. No sense in scaring everyone, she smiled at her reflection in the mirror, and then headed downstairs.

To her surprise, no one was in the kitchen, even though she was positive it was getting close to time for supper. It wasn't like Jacy not to have something on the stove by now, but perhaps she was planning something simple?

"What are you doing down here, young lady?" Drew scolded as he came in the kitchen. "You are supposed to be in bed!"

"I'm hungry," she grinned at him, then took another sip of her milk.

"I would have brought you something," he admonished.

"I'm perfectly capable of getting it myself," she argued, taking another bite of cheese. "Where's Jacy?" she demanded.

"She's upstairs," Drew replied honestly.

"Why? Is she okay?"

"She's in a bit of trouble with Wes, honey. Threw a tantrum..." he explained, knowing better than to try and keep it from her.

"Not over what happened when the Doctor was here?" she asked, filled with guilt.

"No... She's in trouble for several other things, and we really need to stay out of it, Jolie. Hear me?"

"I don't like it, Drew," Jolie declared, her blue eyes full of temper.

"I know you don't, honey," he agreed, then added, "Wes loves Jacy more than life itself. He doesn't enjoy hurting her... just like I don't like it when I have to take you to task for something. I do it because it's necessary to keep peace and harmony between us."

"Is that your way of telling me you haven't changed your mind?" she asked directly.

"I'm going to make it one you won't ever forget, Jolie," he said quietly. "You'd best enjoy sitting while you can, honey, because when the Doctor says it's okay, I'm going to blister your butt good."

"You're acting as though I disobeyed you and went after a bounty. I didn't... I went after my sister... You aren't being fair, Drew!" she argued.

"You risked your life... and I regard that as something very serious. You should have waited for Wes and me, Jolie. Won't do you any good to argue the matter. I'm not going to debate you. And," he added with determination, "I'm not going to debate whether or not you need to be in bed. I'm taking you upstairs and tucking you in, and if you get out of bed again before Doc says you can, I'll add another spanking to the one you have coming."

"You are overbearing!" Jolie told him.

"I'm your husband."

"I don't like you very much right now," she said earnestly.

He grinned, and then swept her off the chair. "I love you, however, and you are going back to bed."

"Would you bring me a book to read?" she asked with a pout.

"Nope. Doc said to rest, and that's what you're going to do."

"Don't bet on it, cowboy," she retorted.

Drew hoped that Jacy's punishment was over, and that Jolie wouldn't hear anything when they walked past their bedroom. He'd play hell to keep her out of it if Jacy was putting up much of a fuss, and he suspected that she wouldn't be able to keep from howling since Wes had used that leather on her. That thing meant business, and he hoped that he'd never have to take it to Jolie.

Fortunately, they made it past Wes and Jacy's bedroom, and down the hallway to theirs. There were times when it was fortuitous to have a couple rooms in between… It gave both couples the privacy they needed… and once Jolie was safely tucked in bed, she wouldn't hear Jacy, unless Jacy screamed down the house. In that case, he'd have to go and put a stop to it himself…!

"Want to come to bed with me?" Jolie asked with a suggestive smile when they entered their room.

"You are supposed to be resting, young lady. That doesn't include making love."

"I'll let you do all the work. I'll just lie here and enjoy it," she teased.

"You are feeling better, aren't you?" he couldn't help chuckling at her.

"I'm fine, Drew... and I really do want to make love..." she purred.

"Not today, honey. If Doc says you're okay tomorrow, then I promise I'll make love to you all you want and then more..."

"Not if you spank me!" she warned him, her eyes snapping.

"I see... Are you saying that if I take you over my knee I'll get a cold shoulder in bed for a while...?" his voice was hard.

"For a good LONG while," she promised. "I don't like being punished, Drew... and if you spank me, you can be sure you won't be touching me until I'm all better...!"

"And that little threat just added another spanking to the mix. Do you want to try for another?" he asked.

"Then it'll be even longer before you'll find me willing," she upped the ante. "I'm not some woman who simpers and accepts your word as the final law, Drew Parker. I'm used to making my own decisions, and I won't be punished for that. You can bet your ass if I think I don't deserve a spanking, and you give me one anyway, I'm going to punish you for it. I daresay you'll cry uncle long before I will!" she kept right on giving him hell.

"That makes three... and before you open your mouth again, you might wish to have a talk with your sister about the leather hanging in the barn. If you sass me one more time, little girl, you'll have your turn with it." He headed for the door, looked over his shoulder, and said, "Keep your butt in that bed, or else!"

****

How on earth was he going to give her forty hearty smacks with his belt? Wes asked himself. Little Jacy was already bruised and marked from the leather, and although it had been over two hours, he was pretty darn sure she was still feeling each one of those stripes.

"Wesley...? Please... may I ask for pardon?" Jacy whimpered, trembling.

She looked so miserable that Wes knew he couldn't go through with it. He dropped his belt, and pulled her up to hold her close. Her little body was shaking, and she started crying. He grabbed a blanket, walked over to the rocking chair and sat down with her on his lap, and wrapped the blanket around her. He stroked her hair, and her back, and continued to rock her after she was sleeping peacefully.

****

"That bump is all gone," Doc smiled. "I don't see one single reason to keep you in bed, young lady, as long as you promise to take it easy for a couple of days."

"What exactly do you mean by 'take it easy', Doc?" Jolie asked.

"It means no hard work, no riding. Just sitting in your rocking chair, letting everyone spoil you a bit. You can do some sewing or reading, and I'd like for you to take a rest in the afternoon for a couple hours. That doesn't sound too hard, does it?" he asked kindly.

"Jolie will do as you say, Doc," Drew promised.

"But I feel fine!" Jolie protested.

"And we want to keep you feeling fine, young lady. If today goes well, you can do a bit more tomorrow. But, if you feel that headache coming back, I want you to send for me. Will you do that, Jolie?" he asked directly.

Jolie caught Drew's expression, and knew better than sass the kindly Doctor. "I'll cooperate," she said reluctantly.

"Good girl."

Jacy, Drew, and even Wes took great pains to see that Jolie was kept occupied and happy. Wes carried a rocking chair into the kitchen so that Jolie could be comfortable and visit with her sister while Jacy baked, and Drew made several trips inside to kiss her and praise her for following the Doctor's orders.

Jolie wasn't used to having people fuss over her, and worry about her. It was making her crazy…!

****

Jolie was going to scream if she didn't get away from her smothering family. She loved them, but she couldn't move without one of them asking what she needed. She needed to be alone for a while.

Drew tucked her in bed for a nap, and the moment he closed the door, Jolie jumped up and quickly pulled on her pants. Her shirt was next, then her socks and boots. She strapped on her gun. She put pillows in the bed, and pulled the blankets up over them. With any luck at all, she would be back before she was missed.

She eased out the window and watched as Drew and Wes rode due east. She waited until they were out of sight, and then jumped out on the tree limb. She was down on the ground in no time, and hurried to the barn. Jacy wouldn't spot her from the kitchen, and she soon had her stallion saddled and mounted, and was on her way.

It felt so good to be free again. She missed being alone sometimes, and not having to answer to anyone else, and not having to worry about their feelings. She also knew how fortunate she was to have a family who loved her. In spite of all

Drew's promises to spank her when she was all better, she was pretty darn sure it was all bluff. He was gradually getting over his scare, and if he did spank her, it wouldn't be all that severe.

Jolie felt her mood lighten as she rode... and knew she could manage to get through another day of pampering now. She smiled, and headed toward the house. She was almost there when the unthinkable happened. A rope dropped over her head and slender shoulders, and dropped to pin her arms to her sides. She was pulled to the ground, and Jolie blacked out when she hit her head.

****

Jacy frowned. The sharp pain in her head wouldn't go away. She staggered to the steps, and made her way upstairs, positive that Jolie was having another of her headaches. She opened the door to Drew and Jolie's bedroom, and hurried to the bed. She pulled back the covers, and discovered that Jolie was missing! The pain in her head was excruciating, and Jacy was sure that Jolie was in trouble of some kind. She went downstairs, and took the rifle from its hiding spot in the kitchen. She went outside and fired off three shots in succession. That would bring Wes and Drew... She sat down on the step and waited.

****

Wes and Drew heard the shots, and were headed back to the house in the next few seconds. "What's wrong?" Wes demanded as he jumped off his horse and ran to where Jacy sat, holding her head.

"It's Jolie. She's gone. I think she's hurt. My head hurts so much... I could feel her migraines, too," Jacy admitted, "but they weren't this bad."

Drew hurried to the barn. "Her stallion is gone."

"She probably rode out right after you did," Jacy said. "Go the opposite way... You'll find her."

"I can't leave you alone, Jacy," Wes argued, helping her up.

"I'll be fine. It's Jolie who needs help, and you need to hurry. I can feel it..." Jacy insisted. "Please, Wes. Go with Drew and find her quickly."

Wes nodded. Jacy wasn't inclined to be dramatic. "I'm with you, brother."

****

"Wake up, damn it!" Jolie sputtered as the cold water hit her in the face. Her head hurt so much, and she was pretty sure she was going to be sick. She fought the nausea, and opened her eyes to see who was tormenting her. She immediately recognized Sam Jones. She'd hauled him in a year ago, and he was sent to prison.

"Yeah, you know me all right." He squatted beside her, playing with his knife. "I warned you what I'd do when I got free."

Jolie lost consciousness again.

Sam swore. He wasn't going to start cutting her until she was awake and he could hear her screams. He walked down to the stream, intent on getting more water to revive her. This revenge wasn't going as he planned!

Jolie tried to clear her head when the water soaked her shirt and face, but it was all she could do to moan. The pain in her head was making her ill, and she couldn't open her eyes. She knew she should be afraid, but nothing really mattered at the moment. She went out again.

Sam was angry. The bitch was spoiling his fun, and he was going to have to shoot her and be off. He couldn't afford to stop long, or the posse would find him. He knew they were close.

****

"Ma'am, are you all right?" the lawman's badge reflected sunlight, and Jacy put her hands over her eyes.

"Yes," she answered.

"We heard shots, and they sounded like they came from here. You know anything about that?" he asked.

"Yes. I made them."

"You shooting at anything in particular?"

Jacy said, "Excuse me. My head is hurting... I called my husband to come. My sister is missing, and I think she's injured."

The lawman stepped down, and helped Jacy inside. "Ma'am, please tell me what's going on. We have an escaped killer on the loose, and if your sister came across him, she's in danger."

****

Sam raised the knife. It would be quieter than a gun, and she would still be one dead bitch! A shot rang out, and Sam was dead before he toppled over.

****

Jolie opened her eyes and smiled in relief. Finally, she would be allowed to live like a normal person. The three weeks had been awful. Her head wouldn't stop pounding, and her body was so bruised from Sam Jones dragging her at the end of the rope. She felt better now, and was thankful to be alive. She glanced at her still sleeping husband, and felt the first tremors of dread invade her thoughts. She knew what Drew had planned for today, and she wasn't looking forward to it... not at all.

He was going to spank her. He'd sworn to it when he found her lying beside the dead killer. At first, he'd thought her dead, too, so she supposed she could permit him to express some of that anguish on her fanny. Once he'd assured himself that she was truly alive, the posse had arrived, and he'd spent several minutes trying to answer their questions while Wes rode to town for the doctor.

The lawman had had a hard time understanding that Jolie had shot and killed the escaped convict when she was barely conscious, until Drew explained about her past as a bounty hunter. Jolie knew that Drew was blaming himself for not getting there in time to rescue her, and she smiled tenderly. She planned to let him take good care of her from now on.

"Good morning," she smiled when he opened his eyes.

"How are you this morning, honey?" he asked, his dark eyes looking her over carefully.

"I'm fine," she responded. "Really and truly fine." She brushed his hair away from his forehead, and then said, "I know you're planning to spank me today, and I know it is deserved... but I would ask that you have a care..."

"I intend to take you to the barn for a proper leathering, Jolie," Drew said firmly.

"I really don't think you will be happy with yourself if you do that, my husband," she argued.

Drew wasn't stupid. He looked at her questioningly. She looked awfully confident for someone in so much trouble with her husband. "Jolie, if you have a valid reason why I shouldn't take you out to the barn, then it's best you speak up here and now. Otherwise, you're going to get the tanning of your life, and I guarantee you're not going to sit for a week."

"I didn't say I didn't deserve a spanking, Drew," Jolie said seriously. "I agree that I went out of my way to earn one, sneaking out of here when I was supposed to be resting... and for scaring you. But, I'm asking you to have a care... I'm with child," she smiled at Drew.

"What? How long have you known?" his eyes were full of joy.

"I suspected some time ago... but when I took the fall from my horse, I was afraid I'd lose the baby. I asked Doc to keep it secret until we knew for sure if I would carry. I'm strong, and so is our baby..." she smiled happily.

Drew was excited, and he took her in his arms and kissed her tenderly, all thoughts of a leathering forgotten. "Do you feel sickness in the mornings?" he asked in a worried tone.

"Nope. I'm all well now, and feeling just great. Doc said I could return to normal today, and," she looked at him in embarrassment, "he said a trip over your knee for a good spanking with a hairbrush wouldn't hurt me or the baby. In fact, he said it was long overdue..." she told the complete truth.

"He said that?" Drew was shocked.

"I asked," she admitted. "I didn't want the baby to suffer... Doc said the baby won't feel a thing, and as long as you support me carefully, it's okay... Could we get it over with now, Drew?" she asked. "I want this behind us so I can start proving to you, and to Jacy and Wes, that I love all of you... and I'm thankful to be a part of this family."

Drew wasn't sure he should spank Jolie, but she wasn't giving him much choice in the matter. She got up and went to the dresser to bring him her hairbrush, and then she climbed on the bed, and lay over his lap. "I know this isn't the leather, but I swear to you I'll be more careful from now on, Drew. And, a hairbrush really hurts..." she added so seriously that he had to smile.

Drew started with his hand, and Jolie took the punishment as quietly as possible, knowing she'd crossed several lines with her husband, and that he was proving in his own sweet way that he loved her. The hairbrush was next, and it wasn't so easy to accept. Her poor bottom was soon flaming and sore, and she was sobbing by the time he finished.

Drew helped her to lie beside him, and cuddled her. "Now hush, young lady. That was a far cry from the leathering I promised you," he teased, "and I want to know when this child of ours is due..."

"It still hurts, honey," she pouted a bit, but was more than happy to talk about the baby...

****

"Are you sure, Jacy?" Wes asked, in awe at the news. "Why haven't you said anything?"

"Because I wanted to be sure..." she smiled happily. "Doc was a bit flustered when I spoke to him... Said, 'If it don't beat all... Twins having babies at the same time...!' I don't think he realized he spoke out loud... Jolie and Drew are expecting too!" she giggled. "You and Drew are going to have to add more rooms to the house!"

Wes let out a whoop of joy...

****

"What was that all about?" Drew looked at his precious wife.

"I imagine Jacy told Wes her good news," Jolie laughed. "She wanted a lighter spankin', too!"

THE END

Blushing Books ® hopes you enjoyed this spicy, spanking novel by Laurel Joseph. We have lots of other erotic novels and novellas available. For the "latest," you may want to check out our Internet websites, owned and operated by our Internet partner, ABCD Webmasters.

Bethany's Woodshed has been publishing erotic and romantic spanking novels since 1998. Each week the website is updated with six new novels or short stories, featuring adult romantic and erotic spanking stories. Every story published on Bethany's Woodshed is original, exclusive, brand-new, and all are written by paid professionals. Bethany's Woodshed is located at:
http://www.herwoodshed.com

Spanking Romance is also a site which is updated weekly. At this site, we publish a completed novella – 4-6 chapters – every week. Again, all stories are brand new and exclusive, written by paid professionals.
Spanking Romance is located at:
http://www.spankingromance.com

Romantic Spankings is our eBook site. On this site there are literally hundreds of eBook novels and novellas, all available for immediate download.
Romantic Spankings is located at:
http://www.romanticspankings.com

Spanking4mykindle is our site promoting Amazon's ebook reader, the Kindle. On this site you can find out more about the Kindle, and also see which of our books are available for instant download to your Kindle.
Spanking4myKindle is located at:
http://www.spanking4mykindle.com

Many of our longer books are also available in print through Amazon. Please check out the following titles:

A Glitch in Time by Judith McClaren ISBN: 978-1-935152-00-2
Master of Wyndham Hall by Sullivan Clarke ISBN: 978-1-935152-01-9
Barbarian Worlds by Sharon Green ISBN: 978-1-935152-02-5
Cindra and The Bounty Hunter by Paige Tyler ISBN: 978-1-935152-03-3
Victorian Brats Volume One by Melinda Barron ISBN: 978-1-935152-04-0
Princess Brat by Sharon Green ISBN: 978-1-935152-05-7
Mistaken by Laurel Joseph ISBN: 978-1-935152-06-4
Magic Spell by Paige Tyler ISBN: 978-1-935152-07-1
The Cutler Brothers by Paige Tyler ISBN: 978-1-935152-08-8
Simple Pleasures by Nattie Jones ISBN: 978-1-935152-09-5
DeAkeny's Bride by Darla Phelps: ISBN: 978-1-935152-10-1
The Friends Series, Volume One by Paige Tyler: ISBN 978-1-935152-11-8
Comanche Canyon, by Judith McClaren: ISBN 978-1-935152-12-5
Second Chances by Carolyn Faulkner: ISBN 978-1-935152-13-2
If You Loved Me by Starla Kaye: ISBN 978-1-935152-14-9
The New Panty Collection by Joannie Kaye: ISBN 978-1-935152-15-6
Last Chance by Joannie Kaye: ISBN 978-1-935152-16-3
Kayla and The Rancher by Paige Tyler: ISBN 978-1-935152-17-0
Samantha and the Detective by Paige Tyler: ISBN 978-1-935152-18-7
Arabella Book One – In Her Lord's Stable by KA Halle: ISBN 978-1-935152-19-4
Spoils of War by Carolyn Faulkner: ISBN 978-1-935152-20-0
Mistaken by Laurel Joseph: ISBN 978-1-935152-06-4

Made in the USA
Lexington, KY
01 December 2009